Fabliaux
Fair & Foul

Translations
by
John DuVal
Introduction and Notes
by
Raymond Eichmann

Pegasus Press
Asheville, North Carolina
1999

For Miller Williams

Earlier versions of some of these fabliaux were published as *Cuckolds, Clerics, & Countrymen: Medieval French Fabliaux* (Fayetteville: University of Arkansas Press, 1982). They are reprinted here courtesy of the Board of Trustees of the University of Arkansas.

© Copyright 1999
Pegasus Press
Asheville, North Carolina

Library of Congress Cataloging-in-Publication Data

Fabliaux, fair and foul / introductions and notes by Raymond Eichmann; translations by John DuVal.
    p. cm.
    Includes bibliographical references.
    ISBN 0-86698-1820-8
    1. French poetry--to1500–Translations into English. 2. Narrative poetry, French--Translations into English. 3. Tales, Medieval--Translations into English. 4. Tales–France--Translations into English. 5. Fabliaux--Translations into English.
I. Eichmann, Raymond. 1943- . II. DuVal, John, 1940-- . III. Title.
PQ1308.E6F3 1992
841'.030901–dc20   91-44327
                                                CIP

This book is made to last.
It is printed on acid-free paper
to library specifications.
Printed in the United States of America

CONTENTS

ABBREVIATIONS

B   Bédier, Joseph. *Les Fabliaux*, 6th ed. Paris: Champion, 1964.

CH Cooke, Thomas D. , and Benjamin L. Honeycutt, eds. *The Humor of the Fabliaux: A Collection of Critical Essays.* Columbia: University of Missouri Press, 1974.

JO Johnston, R. C. , and D. D. R. Owen, eds. *Fabliaux*. Oxford: Basil Blackwell, 1957.

M   Muscatine, Charles. *The Old French Fabliaux*. New Haven and London: Yale University Press, 1986.

MR Montaiglon, Anatole de, and Gaston Raynaud, eds. *Recueil général et complet des fabliaux des XIIIe et XIVe siècles.* 6 vols. Paris, 1872–90; repr. New York: Burt Franklin, n. d. (All references to fabliaux in this text are to volume and page number).

N   Nykrog, Per. *Les Fabliaux: Etude d'histoire littéraire et de stylistique médiévale.* Copenhagen: Munksgaard, 1957.

OF Cooke, Thomas D. *The Old French and Chaucerian Fabliaux: A Study of Their Comic Climax.* Columbia: University of Missouri Press, 1978.

S   Schenck, Mary Jane Stearns. *The Fabliaux. Tales of Wit and Deception.* Purdue University Monographs in Romance Languages, vol. 24. Amsterdam and Philadelphia: John Benjamins, 1987.

Introduction

In the thirteenth century, the medieval French tales which we now call *fabliaux* established themselves as a significant and popular genre. The word *genre* must here be understood in the modern sense as a literary category, for in those times writers were not preoccupied with making neat distinctions among artistic works. Indeed, fabliaux are found widespread among thirty-five manuscripts where medieval collectors and compilers placed them, randomly it appears, alongside epics, courtly romances, lais and lives of saints. Their exact count would depend on the counter's definition of *fabliau* and on whether reworkings (*remaniements*) of the same tale are counted. Thus, Joseph Bédier counted 147 fabliaux; Per Nykrog, 160 (rejecting some from Bédier's list while adding others); and Mary Jane Stearns Schenck, 130.[1] Among all of these, sixty-six tales call themselves *fablel*, the old French word which would have evolved into the modern French *fableau* if scholars hadn't generally preferred *fabliau* from northeastern Picardy, where the tales enjoyed great popularity. One hundred or so other tales are so analogous in composition, narrative tone, or story-line that they may be included in that genre despite the fact that their authors, composers, or narrators call them *dits, dities, aventures, contes, mots, oevres, romans, proverbes, reclaims, livres, exemples,* or *fables.*

DEFINITION

Joseph Bédier's century-old definition of the fabliau as verse tales meant for laughter ("contes à rire en vers," B 30) has the merit of being flexible. The definition is narrow enough to separate the fabliau from other medieval narratives and broad enough to allow pieces which share common characteristics to be included in the canon. The most nearly comprehensive anthology of fabliaux was and is Montaiglon and Raynaud's six volume *Recueil général et complet des fabliaux*

---

[1] Joseph Bédier, *Les Fabliaux*, 6th ed. (Paris: Champion, 1964), 87; Per Nykrog, *Les Fabliaux: Etude d'histoire littéraire et de stylistique médiévale* (Copenhagen: Munksgaard, 1957), 15; Mary Jane Stearns Schenck, *The Fabliaux. Tales of Wit and Deception*, Purdue University Monographs in Romance Languages, vol. 24 (Amsterdam/Philadelphia: John Benjamins, 1987), 63.

des XIIIe et XIVe siècles (1872–90).[1] Bédier's definition allowed for almost all of the 157 works in that anthology, but excluded some short tales which were not comic, as well as some comic speeches which were not tales. It also allowed for the huge variety in the length of the tales, which range from the eighteen-line *Le Prestre et le mouton* (*The Priest and the Sheep*, MR 6:109) to the 1364-line *Le Prestre et le chevalier* (*The Priest and the Knight*, MR 2:46). The second longest is a 1,164-line version of our *The Sacristan Monk* called *Le Prestre qu'on porte* (*The Priest Who is Carried*, MR 4:1) aptly subtitled *La Longue Nuit* (*The Long Night*). The opening lines of *Aloul*, the longest tale in this collection, seem to be preparing the audience for a longer tale than usual. Indeed, the tales average between 300 and 400 lines, all in octosyllabic couplets.

Per Nykrog's stipulation that the tale must confine itself to the narration of a single episode and its immediate results supplements Bédier's definition by clarifying the term *conte*, or *story*.

Other attempts at defining the fabliau fail to improve on Bédier's. Knud Togeby has built an elaborate table of narrative genres wherein most medieval works are categorized according to levels, lengths, and attitudes. The fabliau, for him, is a low-level thirteenth-century short story ("nouvelle de niveau bas du XIIIème siècle").[2] This definition suffers in comparison to Bédier's because "low-level" is even less objective than "meant for laughter," and because limiting the fabliaux to a one-hundred-year existence is needlessly arbitrary, whereas Bédier's criterion that they must be verse is supported by the texts themselves.

Thomas Cooke adds to our understanding of the nature of the fabliau by arguing that what unites the disparate tales is the artistic preparation for the climax and the reader/listener's enjoyment at finding his or her anticipation fulfilled.[3] In his structural approach, Cooke does not insist on defining the genre on the basis of this charac-

---

[1] Anatole de Montaiglon and Gaston Raynaud, eds., *Recueil général et complet des fabliaux des XIIIe et XIVe siècles* (Paris, 1872–1990; repr. New York: Burt Franklin, n. d.). Here and hereafter, all references to a fabliau are cited by volume and page number. *Trubert*, which has 2986 lines, although a self-proclaimed fabliau, has been correctly recategorized as a "roman" or "conte picaresque" by Nykrog (15) and Schenck (68). A comprehensive edition of the fabliaux is currently in progress: Willem Noomen and Nico van den Boogaard, eds., *Nouveau Recueil complet des fabliaux*, 4 vols. (Assen: Van Gorcum, 1983–88).

[2] "The Nature of the Fabliaux," in *The Humor of the Fabliaux: A Collection of Critical Essays*, ed. Thomas D. Cooke and Benjamin L. Honeycutt (Columbia: University of Missouri Press, 1974), 9.

[3] Thomas D. Cooke, *The Old French and Chaucerian Fabliaux: A Study of Their Comic Climax* (Columbia: University of Missouri Press, 1978), 162–69.

teristic because it is not a feature unique to the fabliau, and he is, in fact, comfortable with Bédier's definition.

One would think that the surest way to define the fabliau is to follow Bédier's recommendation and search for analogous traits among all the fabliaux which bear that name and to accept as fabliaux other tales which also possess those traits (B 30). The problem, as Willem Noomen and Jean Rychner have pointed out, is that the process of finding analogies rests on one's choices of criteria, and so we can hope for little more than circular definitions: Bédier examines certain texts, discovers characteristics which most have in common, and defines *fabliau* according to those characteristics; we who come after determine what texts are fabliaux according to Bédier's definition.

Willem Noomen also analyzed the self-named fabliaux and concluded that the fabliaux are brief narratives in octosyllabic couplets whose protagonists are human beings and that each fabliau is an independent tale, that is, not part of a vaster structure. For each of these criteria, however, there is at least one exception, at least one self-proclaimed fabliau which does not conform.[1]

Mary Jane Stearns Schenck also based her analysis of sixty-six tales expressly called *fabliaux* and extracted nine Proppian functions common to sixty of them.[2] The common elements in all these fabliaux are the narrative functions of arrival, departure, interrogation, communication, deception, misdeed, recognition, retaliation, and resolution. Her morphological effort to define the boundaries of the genre and to apply them to the other poems in the Montaiglon-Raynaud collection generally considered as fabliaux revealed that eighteen of those poems, in addition to six self-proclaimed fabliaux, must be rejected from the corpus of fabliaux. This process leaves us with 130 tales which can be assumed, with the greatest degree of certainty, to be fabliaux whose definition is as follows: "A fabliau is a brief narrative poem with a tripartite macrostructure whose narrative is a humorous, even ribald, story arranged to teach a lesson" (S 36). She clarifies that definition by stipulating that the narratives are about trickery and changes in fortune and that the morals contain "warnings about deceptions and a secular system of punishment" (S 36).

All these additional precisions and refinements to Bédier's definition are noteworthy, but do make that definition unnecessarily cumber-

---

[1] Willem Noomen, "Qu'est-ce qu'un fabliau?" in *XIV Congresso internazionale di linguistica e filologia romanza*, ed. Alberto Várvaro (Naples: Macchiaroli, 1981), 425–27. We must keep in mind that several poems which call themselves fabliaux are not narrative, but are mere declamations. Hence the few exceptions (ten) to the categories.

[2] Schenck, 40–64. Schenck recognizes that some fabliaux use only six functions, ending the narrative after the sixth (56).

some. Bédier's definition seems always to pass the test of critics who end up accepting it although they would like it to be more discriminating and more refined. For our purposes here, the fabliaux are verse tales meant for laughter.

POPULARITY AND ORIGINS

The fabliaux were undoubtedly very popular in their day. Not only were they given the honor of being written down on parchment instead of on ephemeral wax tablets, but several have been transmitted to us in a number of manuscripts. *Auberee* appears in eight manuscripts; the *Sacristan* stories are related in eight versions; others like our own *The Maiden Who Couldn't Hear* . . . and *The Butcher of Abbeville* in five; *The Wife of Orleans, The Tresses, Hearmie,* and many other fabliaux in three.

But where did this popular genre come from? Because of striking resemblances between some fabliaux and Oriental tales, Theodor Benfey contended that all the narrative elements came from India by way of the Crusaders or the Spanish Moors.[1] In 1874, Benfey's theory of the Oriental origin of the fabliaux was restated by Gaston Paris, who was to bear the brunt of subsequent attacks. In 1895 Bédier masterfully demolished the theory, demonstrating that to attempt to discover a common geographical source for all tales was futile and that the tales were part of the legacy of mankind. According to Bédier, it was the specifically Gallic genius that molded the raw material into its artistic form. Bédier noted that the fabliau flourished concomitantly with the rise of a middle class, neither aristocratic nor peasant, of craftsmen, money lenders, and merchants (mostly townsmen, or *burghers*), called the *bourgeoisie*; and he concluded that the fabliau was the creation of this new class and that fabliaux were written by and for the bourgeoisie, despite evidence that the aristocracy also had a taste for them, too.

In 1957 the Danish scholar Per Nykrog attacked Bédier's thesis that the fabliau was a bourgeois genre. True, Nykrog pointed out, the fabliaux appeared around the time of the emergence of the bourgeois class, but so did the courtly romance (N xl–xli). Equating style with audience, Nykrog maintained that the fabliau was an aristocratic genre, written for the aristocracy and, possibly, for the highest order of the bourgeoisie.[2] In returning the fabliaux to the aristocracy, he rehabilitated them. Whereas Bédier had hastily judged them unworthy of consid-

---

[1] For a good summary of this question, see Nykrog, xx–xxxviii.

[2] This advice is echoed by Jean Rychner, "Les Fabliaux: Genre, styles, publics," in *La Littérature narrative d'imagination,* Colloque de Strasbourg, 1959 (Paris: Presses Universitaires de France, 1961), 41–54.

eration and, for the most part, without artistic merit, the medieval manuscript collectors, Nykrog pointed out, deemed them worthy to be placed alongside highly artistic romances and epics. The fabliau, for him, is "très souvent une parodie de la courtoisie, mais loin de viser l'aristocratie, cette parodie se moque des classes qui lui sont inférieures" (very often a parody of courtliness, but far from being aimed at the aristocracy, this parody makes fun of the lower classes, N 104). In Nykrog's estimation, the nobility amused themselves at the expense of "la courtoisie des vilains" (the courtliness of the commoners, N 104). Knud Togeby agreed and expanded his definition to include parody of serious courtly genres (CH 8-9).

Charles Muscatine also disagreed with Bédier and, on the basis of vocabulary analysis, found evidence that the fabliaux have a rural, not a burgher character.[1] Unlike Nykrog, however, he concluded that, in view of the nonhomogeneity of medieval social classes, the fabliaux could not be the property of one lone class.

An entirely different theory of origins had earlier come from the noted classicist Edmond Faral who, in 1924, argued that the dramatic nature of ancient Latin comedies by Plautus and Terence had been totally misunderstood by the medieval authors who had transformed them into narrative fiction.[2] The fabliaux, he claimed, had their origin in the written, medieval Latin comedy, which would make them the possession of the clerical, learned class. But why then, Nykrog correctly objected, do no fabliaux preserve from those Latin comedies any stylistic traits, any stock characters, such as the lazy slave, the glutton, the braggart soldier, or the knavish servant? A more likely link exists between medieval drama and the fabliaux, which were often acted out in what Grace Frank calls "représentation par personnages."[3] This confusion of genres led Faral to mistake a clearly dramatic thirteenth-century play such as *Courtois d'Arras* for a fabliau acted out in front of an audience.[4] The dramatic nature of the fabliau does not necessarily imply a formal relationship between the two genres beyond the fact that they share some common themes which probably were circulating in written or oral forms at the time.

R. C. Johnston and D. D. R. Owen, as well as Nykrog, have suggested that the fabliau might have originated from fables.[5] Etymologi-

---

[1] "The Social Background of the Old French Fabliaux," *Genre* 9 (1976): 1-19.

[2] Edmond Faral, "Le Fabliau latin au moyen âge," *Romania* 50 (1924): 321-85.

[3] Grace Frank, *The Medieval French Drama*, 3d ed. (Oxford: Clarendon Press, 1987), 213-14.

[4] Edmond Faral, ed. , *Courtois d'Arras*, C. F. M. A. (Paris: Champion, 1961), iii-iv.

[5] R. C. Johnston and D. D. R. Owen, eds., *Fabliaux* (Oxford: Basil Blackwell, 1957), xiii-xviii.

cally and thematically, the link between fables and fabliaux can be accepted: certainly tales such as *De Plaine Bourse de sens* (*The Purse Full of Sense*, MR 3:67) and *De La Housse partie* (*The Blanket that was Divided*, MR 1:82), accepted by Bédier, but excluded by Nykrog (N 94), have, like the fables, a moralistic intent so pronounced that it overshadows any feeble attempt at comedy. Our own *Browny, The Priest's Cow* and *Greed and Envy* (both self-proclaimed fabliaux) resemble the short, light Aesopic tales. This theory has the merit of not linking the fabliau to a particular social class and makes the fable the point of departure for the fabliau (N 252). The stories, the timeless raw material of funny tales and bawdy jokes, were modified and moralized by the much shorter fables, some of which could even be considered, as Nykrog put it, "fabliaux avant la lettre" (fabliaux before the term, N 251–55). Under its own impetus, as its popularity grew and as it established itself as a genre, the fabliau outgrew the moralistic purpose and allowed the moral to become optional. Laughter prevailed over instruction, which, even when kept, could be delivered tongue in cheek.

The universality of fabliau material cannot be overstressed. Some of the fabliaux can be attributed to certain social classes, but Muscatine cautions that social classes were more mobile than Bédier had supposed. France's social makeup was very complex in the Middle Ages, and outside of Paris, the social distinctions between country people and burghers were often blurred.[1] Nor can a unique literary source be discovered for the fabliaux. Each of the fabliaux must be considered individually, and no one social class or literary genre will reveal the secret of their origin.

AUDIENCE

Often the issues of origin and audience are blurred. Joseph Bédier assigned the fabliaux to bourgeois audiences, although he admitted the aristocracy's liking for the genre. Nykrog claimed that since only the upper class was familiar with courtly literature, only the upper class could truly enjoy the parodic nature of the fabliaux.[2] He erred in

---

[1] "The Social Background," 18, 19. See also Marie-Thérèse Lorcin, *Façons de sentir et de penser: Les Fabliaux français* (Paris: Champion, 1979), 17–20.

[2] On the subject of the parody of courtly and epic genres, both Jean Subrenat in "Notes sur la tonalité des fabliaux," *Marche Romane* 25 (1975): 83–94, and Roy J. Pearcy in "Chansons de Geste and Fabliaux: 'La Gageure' and 'Bérengier au long cul,'" *Neuphilologische Mitteilungen* 79 (1978): 76–83, support Nykrog's thesis. L. -F Flutre, in "Le Fabliau, genre courtois," in *Frankfurter Universitätsreden* 22 (1960): 70–84, cautions against too much of an exclusive and systematized usage of this theory.

assuming that a degree of sophistication implies an aristocratic audience. Like Nykrog, Jean Rychner advised strongly to look at the style, "c'est le style, non le sujet, qui jauge le niveau social d'une oeuvre" (it is the style, not the subject, that indicates the social level of a work).[1] Examining variant versions of a number of fabliaux, he invariably assumed that the best written were the earliest and the ones destined for a higher class audience, whereas the more poorly written ones were, in his view, revised and adapted for a less demanding (in other words, bourgeois and popular) public. However, from the tales themselves, we can gather that the audiences were mixed. Some fabliaux must have been recited in taverns, for one jongleur (*Du Povre Mercier, The Poor Haberdasher,* MR 2:122) asks, "Done moi boire, si t'agree" (please pour me a drink!). Others were performed at market places, in castles, and, in one case at least, at the house of an individual (*De Boivin de Provins,* MR 5:52), where it was the custom to have the guest recite a fabliau when invited to stay over. Johnston and Owen state, "It would be unwise to allot to them one particular public as it would be to ascribe them solely to one class or author" (JO vi). A natural temptation would be to assume that each fabliau is destined for the social class of its most sympathetic character or destined to the class furthest from that of its least sympathetic character. Based on that principle, because the peasants in *De La Sorisete des Etopes* (*The Little Mouse from Oakum,* MR 4:158) and *Del Fol Vilain* (*The Crazy Peasant*) are so pitifully ignorant, those fabliaux would be intended for a noble or upper-middle class and a third version of the same story (*Du Sot Chevalier, The Foolish Knight,* MR 1:200), which makes the sexual ignoramus a knight, would be intended for a lower class.[2] But such an assumption neglects the fact that most people are able to laugh at themselves and that they can enjoy laughing at the types of people they know best, including the people of their own class.

---

[1] Jean Rychner, *Contribution à l'étude des fabliaux: Variantes, remaniements, dégradations,* 2 vols. (Geneva: Droz, 1960), 58.

[2] *Del Fol Vilain* is published in Charles H. Livingston's *Le Jongleur Gautier le Leu* (Cambridge: Harvard University Press, 1951), 147–58. Krystyna Kasprzyk, "Pour la sociologie du fabliau: Convention, tactique, et engagement," *Kwartalnik Neofilologiczny* 23 (1976): 153–61, restates well the problems of attributing fabliaux to a specific social class. Interestingly, *Del Fol Vilains* and *Del Sot Chevalier* (Livingston, 187–97), are both from Gautier le Leu and show no substantial differences in "style" either. Attributing a different audience to these tales on the basis of characters or style as Rychner does, is, therefore, very problematic.

THE MULTIPLE LIVES OF A FABLIAU

The tale of the foolish peasant/knight is one of many tales with multiple versions. In fact, since an appreciable percentage of the fabliaux appear in more than one manuscript, it is rare for there not to be differences in wording. Some texts, although retelling the same story (our *Du Bouchier d'Abevile* and *Du Prestre et du chevalier, The Priest and the Knight,* MR 2:46) can be considered separate tales, while others are so closely related that they can only be regarded as copies of one another. Thus, the study of interdependency of the various tales is a very complex one, for there must have been a substantial gap between the time of composition and performance of a work and its transcription to a manuscript. Johnston and Owen's explanation that "scribes felt free to abridge, to expand, to alter details or facts, and to improve stylistically on the story they retold" (JO xx) is better applied to those who spread the tale orally, the jongleurs, who constantly recreated it from performance to performance. These jongleurs were freelance performers who entertained with trained animals, juggling, songs, epics, and fabliaux. Because their livelihood depended on the success of each performance, they had a deeper commitment than scribes would have had to each poem as their own poem. Each fabliau had to be the best they could make it in accordance with their abilities as performers, with what jokes worked best for them, and what particular plot best stirred their particular audiences.

The jongleur, with his versatile talents, his ability to recompose tales at will, is one element, but perhaps not the only one, accounting for the multiplicity of variant versions of fabliaux. There existed in medieval times veritable copying factories which Bédier called *ménestrandies* and whose functions were at once artistic and commercial. Copyists would either copy as faithfully as possible the original works or change passages either out of boredom or a desire to improve on them. This process implies written composition, the presence of another book before one's eyes. Nykrog, however, argues that since no surviving manuscripts show identical canons of works, the impact of such copying factories is purely conjectural (N 39–50).

Furthermore, the oral nature of the fabliaux is undeniable in view of the numerous calls to attention (e. g. , "My lords, if you will linger here / A little while and lend an ear" [*The Three Hunchbacks,* ll. 1–2]), of the calls for an audience to make a judgment (*The Butcher of Abbeville,* ll. 568–74), and of the appeals to the hearing sense ("Listen," "hear," and so on). Asides such as the one by the "author" of *Estormi* (MR 1:198) point to the oral nature of the fabliaux: "Mais je ne sais par quoi ce fu, / Quar onques conté ne me fu" (I don't know how this was, / For I never was told). Obviously, jongleurs — not scribes — asked for drinks in *Du Povre Mercier* and in *Du Mantel Mautaillé* (MR 3:321, "Or, vous, donez boivre du vin!" (Hey! You! Pour some wine!). It is indeed difficult to argue against the orality of a performance or against the oral transmission of tales.

Jean Rychner's theory of the origins of the epic probably applies better to the fabliau than does his later theory that the variant fabliaux are the results of *dégradations mémorielles* or of too hasty copying. Any version of any epic, according to Rychner, indicates one oral stage of the song, and those stages vary from performance to performance.[1] If differences exist, they are due to spontaneous composition during declamation. Every version of a tale which we have in written form is, in fact, a sort of stenographic recording of a piece at a certain stage of that piece's circulation. Thematic and "textual" similarities and differences can thus be explained. Like the epic texts, the variant fabliau texts are probably records of individual oral performances. For instance, the fabliau *De Boivin de Provins*, mentioned above, was declaimed in front of an audience on more than one occasion: "Souvent li fist conter sa vie / A ses parents, a ses amis" (Often he had him retell his adventure / To his relatives and his friends, MR 5:64). Boivin was invited to stay three whole days and asked to repeat his performance. And he was well paid for it:

Se li dona de ses deniers
Li provos . X. sous a Boivins
Qui fist cest fablel a Provins. (MR 5:64)

Thus the provost gave of his money,
10 sous, to Boivin
Who "made" this fabliau at Provins.

This provost certainly sounds like Nykrog's collector (N 47–50). Having heard a good story, the collector would request its transcription on a wax tablet or loose parchment sheet. Later, when his private holdings increased, he would have a copyist rewrite them and bind the volume. This explanation accounts not only for variants found in other manuscripts, since the dictated text is essentially an individual oral tale recorded at a particular time, but also for the fact that tales never appear in the same order in any two manuscripts. We must, therefore, not lose sight of the oral processes of composition and of performance which make a certain tale one way in one version and different in another.

---

[1] Jean Rychner, *La Chanson de Geste: Essai sur l'art épique des jongleurs* (Geneva: Droz, 1955).

THE MESSAGE OF THE FABLIAUX

The fabliau is a very mobile and, therefore, a very elusive genre, and the search for origins and influences, a favorite pastime for critics, is made particularly arduous by the difficulties in establishing an evolutionary chain of tales. The precise audience seems equally elusive: whether the tales were composed for and by the bourgeois class or whether, as courtly burlesques, they were the appanage of aristocratic courtly literature may never be decided. Mary Jane Stearns Schenck notes that in the self-proclaimed fabliaux, although the commoners in the fabliaux outnumber the members of any other class by about two to one, there is an amazingly even distribution of characters from the aristocracy, the clergy, and the bourgeoisie (S 71). She praises Charles Muscatine for having pointed out that the ability to understand the fabliaux' message lies not in the determination of what social class they were destined for, but of what social forces were at work in those times which the fabliaux celebrated.[1] Muscatine demonstrated that the fabliau era was witness to a commercial revolution which opened up opportunities to those who were clever and eager for profit. Unfortunately for his thesis, Muscatine believed that the attitudes which social mobility encouraged were bourgeois, low-level, and unworthy, infecting the whole of society (M 111). Schenck, on the other hand, sees this social mobility as a much more positive force, which the fabliaux celebrate: an ethos of profit, cleverness yes, but also an emphasis on intelligence, spontaneity, reason, ambition, quick-wittedness, and practicality. "Mielz valt engiens que ne fait force" (Trickery is worth more than brute strength—*Du Vilain qui conquist Paradis par plait, The Peasant Who Took Paradise by Debate*, MR 3:81), she quotes to demonstrate the new perception, the celebration of shrewdness which would elevate the *Laboratores* (those who work), if they be wise, to the status of the *Oratores* (those who pray) or the *Bellatores* (those who fight). We can certainly point to our *Lai of Aristotle* as a poem praising intelligence and warning of the dangers when emotions and feelings obscure even an intelligent man's reasoning.

Schenck also points out the importance of money in obtaining status. The new peasantry, armed with intelligence and the tools of their new crafts, is superior to those whom Marie-Thérèse Lorcin calls

---

[1] Schenck, 109-20, more succinctly stated in "The Fabliaux Ethos: Recent Views on its Origins," *Reinardus*, Yearbook of the International Reynard Society, ed. Brian Levy and Paul Wackers, vol. 1 (Grave: Alfa, 1988), 121-29. Charles Muscatine's views have been synthesized in his *The Old French Fabliaux* (New Haven and London: Yale University Press, 1986), especially 73-104.

"les hommes arrivés," the establishment.[1] This new class, which has specialized knowledge and tools and which includes butchers, artisans, blacksmiths, brewers, fishermen, bakers, money-changers, healers and millers — all prestigious professions in the fabliaux — is pitted not only against the slower-witted peasants, but also against those "en place" who have an interest in denouncing profit and ambition as disruptive of the natural order. Our tale of *The Villager and His Two Asses*, with its recommendation not to try to rise above one's condition, stands as a rare example of such defensive attitudes, although it is quite evident, in this brief tale, that the Villager does not belong to the new grouping of prestigious professions mentioned above. The recommendation in that moral seems to imply that one should not attempt to get ahead unless one has the necessary tools, professional as well as intellectual: pride and ambition alone, without "sens et mesure," do not guarantee success.

According to Schenck, therefore, the fabliaux capture the energy of their time and preach an attitude of confidence in the probability of social ascent through what she calls "an ethos of practicality, ambition, and celebration of quick-wittedness" (S 116). The very same ethic is found in another related popular genre, the *Roman de Renart*.

Such a seriousness of intent must be emphasized in order to correct a misconception about the fabliaux that has existed for a long time. Bédier considered them "amusettes," short entertaining tales having little to do with reality and devoid of instructional purpose (B 311). Even Nykrog treated them only as counterparts to the more serious genres. Schenck corrects this misconception by noting that seventy percent of the self-proclaimed fabliaux conclude, directly or secondarily, with some sort of moral, proverb, or judgment. For her, the serious intent of the fabliaux cannot be challenged, for humor is only a vehicle: the fabliaux provide comic examples in order to teach the audiences to exercise intellectual vigilance against those who deceive (especially women), and to be wise with their money and with their choice of friends (S 20; 30–32).

THE VALUE OF THE FABLIAUX

At the basis of the critics' refusal to allow any serious purpose to the fabliau is perhaps their reluctance to admit literary value beyond a few isolated brilliant passages. "Ce qui frappe d'abord c'est l'absence de toute prétention littéraire chez nos auteurs" (What is most immediately striking is the absence of all literary pretension among our authors), says Bédier in a superficial chapter on the fabliaux' style (B 341).

---

[1] *Façons de sentir*, 186.

Nykrog, however, argues that the medieval manuscript writers and collectors themselves evidently did not consider the fabliaux artistically base. In the manuscripts, the fabliaux keep good company alongside "respectable" romances, lais, and moral tales. Rutebeuf, Jean Bodel, Jean de Condé, Philippe de Beaumanoir, and Henri d'Andeli, among others, were prominent poets who did not think it beneath themselves to write fabliaux. Moreover, a closer look at these poems shows that a great deal of artistic skill often did go into their creation. The octosyllabic rhymed couplet, a verse form of some reputation and tradition, gives the fabliau a brisk jaunty rhythm. Since the fabliau is a short narrative and must proceed to its conclusion, the couplet provides a staccato, uninterrupted rhythm. The ear learns to respond to the couplet rhythm so that the listeners are constantly anticipating the second line, and when it comes, they feel the pleasure of fulfilled expectancy and often discover a key word or a new twist of meaning. In *The Priest Who Peeked*, the priest finishes the assault on the peasant's wife before the husband can understand what has happened and before the listener can dwell on the tale's erotic quality. The verse has hurried the tale to its conclusion and left no time for any response but laughter. When the lady in *Berangier of the Long Ass* reveals to her husband who it is who will protect her from him for the rest of her life, the octosyllable allows her to relish the triumph of her revelations: "Berangier" she says, lingering over the last syllable because it is the end of a line (and rhyming with *dangier* in the original), even though his name is only half the hero's full title. Then "Au long cul" (Of the Long Ass) comes down hard, abrupt, sudden, and emphatically punctuated by the early pause at the end of *cul* (ll. 286–87).

In *The Butcher of Abbeville*, the conversations between the lady, the servant girl, and the priest are more than mere squabbles. However nasty the separate speeches may be, once linked together in the couplet form, they click with ping-pong rapidity. This click, which is as pleasurable to the ear of the audience as it is painful to the participants, is a product of the meaning, the meter, the rhyme, and the fact that the dialogue usually shifts in the middle of a couplet (ll. 417–64).

One quality that Bédier praised the fabliau for was its brevity (B 347). A quality, but also a restriction! There is little opportunity to elaborate or develop characters in a brief tale. The fableor has to present straightforwardly the necessary elements of his tale. Paul Theiner shows how all the other elements are reduced to bare functional necessity as the fabliau concentrates on its single purpose, which is that of amusing its audience; little decorative description can be allowed lest the public's attention be diverted from this purpose.[1]

---

[1] Paul Theiner, "Fabliau Settings," in *CH* 119–36.

Whatever ornamental richness there is will have to be extended by the procedure of allusion, as, for example, the courtly description of the lady in *The Three Hunchbacks* (ll. 16–24).

Another consequence of the fabliau's brevity is the lack of opportunity for character development. The characters are painted as types, stock figures: they often remain unnamed, as in *Berangier*. While modern writers often juxtapose the most dominant personality traits, for instance, the dreamer versus the man of action, the fabliau, according to Nykrog, juxtaposes outward features (N 109). The peasant is opposed to the priest, the lover to the husband, the beautiful wife to her old, sometimes ugly, husband. Nykrog elaborates a rigorous chart outlining the various possibilities of opposition among characters and leaving the impression that a character's nature and actions are rigidly predictable: a priest is punished in two-thirds of his attempted seductions and is never successful when the husband is a knight (N 110). The predictability of the fabliau is easily understandable in view of the oral nature and presentation of tales whose success is based on immediate, or near-immediate, recognition by the audience. Cooke, however, modifies the impression of rigidity left by Nykrog's figures. Granting that the fabliau characters are not as fully developed as those of other genres, he demonstrates that they are more than types (OF 24–40): although fableors wish to present them as quickly as possible, they still add many complexities that enrich personalities and situations alike. Clearly, the fabliaux have artistic merits that are coming to light more and more under unprejudiced scrutiny.

The most pernicious and damaging legacy of Bédier is the assumption that the fabliaux are mere "risées," "gabets" (jeers, jokes, B 303), devoid of serious thought. These labels have stuck for many years and critics have been satisfied to note only the entertaining function of our tales, thought to "offer relaxation and refreshment rather than spiritual understanding."[1] Lately, however, new insights into some individual tales have pointed toward the more serious function of conveying important meaning, for instance, the new ethos which Schenck describes. Earlier, Roy J. Pearcy had shown that the fabliaux' humor probably arose from "basic, preconscious habits of mind" rather than the "conflict between the Aristotelian point of view the authors espouse and the Augustinian Neoplatonism they reject."[2] He agrees, broadly, with Schenck that the tales promote a materialistic, analytical, and concrete mentality over the speculative and idealistic one; in other

---

[1] Glending Olson, "The Medieval Theory of Literature for Refreshment and Its Use in the Fabliau Tradition," *Studies in Philology* 71 (1974): 291–313.

[2] Roy J. Pearcy, "Modes of Signification and the Humor of Obscene Diction in the Fabliaux," in *CH* 169.

words, nominalism over realism (CH 194–95). Howard Helsinger advises us to read the fabliaux beyond the literal level by analyzing several other levels of meanings, such as the allegorical levels in *The Butcher of Abbeville, The Partridges,* and others.[1]

Some fabliaux (such as *The Butcher of Abbeville*) might carry a message additional to the storyline or to the stated moral, and some of these messages are communicated to the audience in a nonliteral transmission.[2] We are often alerted to possibilities of different levels of understanding and to the possiblity of traveling from one level to another thanks to the pliable nature of language. Note, for instance, the fabliau's playful attitude toward words and language in *Browny, the Priest's Cow,* where the literal understanding of a message is, to everybody's amazement and amusement, proven correct. Words do convey more than their literal meaning. In the fabliau, a goose is not only a goose, but also a signal that lovemaking, with all its subsequent complexities, is imminent. Likewise, a bath is not only a bath, but always a prelude to the illicit game of love and a signal that we can expect the "unexpected" return of the husband. We laugh at the double-entendre of the fabliau *The Partridges* where the husband chases the priest/lover with a sharp knife. He believes the priest has eaten all the birds while the latter fears he intends to castrate him: "You are carrying them off good and hot / You'll leave them here if I catch you," the husband yells. As Helsinger shrewdly remarks, partridges were notoriously lecherous birds in medieval bestiaries, and it is right for the priest, having led a spiritually sterile life, to "fear literal castration" (CH 96). The malleable nature of words, their polyvalence, allows again the figurative to be presented in a literal, concrete narrative.

Let us consider, lastly, the marvelous fabliau of *William of the Falcon.* This tale is in fact a courtly lai until line 514, when it turns into a fabliau at the precise moment when the pliable nature of words is discovered.[3] William, a young squire, is literally starving to death because his lady refuses to give herself to him. Given the option of either committing adultery or causing someone's death, she explains to her husband that William is dying of sorrow for not being granted a prized possession of his. She means herself, but under the brutal questioning of her husband, she claims that he desires his most pre-

---

[1] Howard Helsinger, "Pearls in the Swill, Comic Allegory in the French Fabliaux," in *CH* 93–105.

[2] Raymond Eichmann, "The Her(m)ites of the 'Bouchier d' Abevile'," *South Central Review* 2, no. 4 (1985): 1–7.

[3] Raymond Eichmann, "The Failure of Literary Language in 'Guillaume au Faucon'," in *Reinardus,* Yearbook of the International Reynard Society, ed. Brian Levy and Paul Wackers, vol. 1 (Grave: Alfa, 1988), 72–78.

cious falcon instead. The lady gets out of her moral impasse by having her husband, a consummate literalist, give William his *faucon* (an insidious play on the words *faux con*, i. e. , false pudendum). Reality and morality have been exorcised by words: "Now you have your falcon / Two half crowns are a crown, I reckon. / And she was right; one thing—two words / One word would get him two rewards" (ll. 575–78). It is precisely this art of "one thing—two words" which presupposes a certain amount of intelligence and characterizes many fabliaux. One observes in the fabliaux a consciousness of the artificiality of language, especially literary language, and its dubious efficacy as a vehicle of communication, but also, and perhaps more importantly in view of the overall light tone of the tales, one notes the exhilaration at the discovery that words are not limited to a one-to-one relationship with meaning. Noomen points out that the fabliaux' narrative schemes center on not only a misidentification of persons, behavior or objects, but also on what he calls "une rupture dans le fonctionnement normal du circuit de la communication" (a break in the normal functioning of the communication circuit).[1] The liberties which both narrators and characters take with language are the greatest source of laughter.

In the fabliau, everything is subservient to laughter. Johnston and Owen stress the macabre humor in the fabliau (JO ix): the audience is made to laugh at physical deformities (hunchbacks), infirmities (blindness), or corpses that are carried from place to place. For Bédier, the comic is superficial and easily achieved (B 313). This notion has been severely shaken by modern critics, who have shown that humor is often complex and its climax artistically prepared. The fableors achieve humor by conscious ploys, either by establishing distance between the characters and the public, or by blatant parody and burlesque. They also create an ironic vision, which most essayists in Cooke and Honeycutt's *The Humor of the Fabliaux* have analyzed. The importance of these essays is that they demonstrate the sophistication of the fableor's comic devices and rehabilitate the genre, placing it on the artistic level of other medieval works. If indeed Norris Lacy is correct in pointing out that humor is primarily achieved by a technique of distancing that frees the audience from any dangerous sympathetic attachment to the characters, then we can begin to accept, even humorously, the "macabre" elements of the fabliaux.[2]

Why did the fabliaux disappear in the middle of the fourteenth century? It is not a coincidence that jongleurs and fabliaux faded away concurrently. The early jongleur was not only a poet; he was an acrobat, an animal trainer, a dancer, an actor, a juggler, and a fire-eater.[3]

---

[1] "Qu'est-ce qu'un fabliau?" 428.

[2] Norris J. Lacy, "Types of Esthetic Distance in the Fabliaux," in *CH* 107–17.

[3] On the jongleurs, see Edmond Faral, *Les Jongleurs en France au moyen âge*

Those talented and versatile performers were often violently condemned by the church because of their dissolute lives and their reputation for leading others, including clerics, into sin. Traveling around the
country, they were highly popular among thirteenth century audiences
of all levels. Later, as the supply of jongleurs increased, the demand for
them slackened. Those particularly gifted and fortunate found steady
patronage among the nobility and were called minstrels (*minister*:
servant at court). In this servile function, they had to specialize in the
more noble types of endeavors: some became men of letters, while
others specialized in other artistic functions as actors, singers, or
musicians. It was the jongleurs, with their versatility and their relative
freedom, who were instrumental in spreading the fabliaux. Once they
disappeared, the fabliaux were replaced by prose tales such as *Les XV
Joies de Mariage*, and *Les Cent Nouvelles Nouvelles*. The often anonymous jongleurs were replaced by writers of such renown as Marguerite
de Navarre and Nicolas de Troyes.

Certainly Chaucer and Boccaccio owed a great debt to our little
tales without ever crediting them as sources. France, Italy, and England
are geographically close, and oral tales travel fast and easily. Both
writers use plots and characters similar to those in the fabliaux and
share their comic spirit and lively style. Indeed, some of the tales, such
as *The Wife of Orleans*, find close analogues in Boccaccio, while
Chaucer's *Shipman's Tale* and *Miller's Tale* are very close to being
typical fabliaux. The common fund of stories from which the materials
were drawn never exhausted itself, and the fabliau enjoyed a brief
revival with Jean de La Fontaine in the seventeenth century. The fabliau
will certainly never die in spirit: a good story is as eternal as the air we
breathe (probably as polluted, too). The raw material continues to exist;
but the art of rhyming has unfortunately been neglected. That neglect
is one of the reasons for the present volume.

With these twenty fabliaux, we hope to give an idea of the variety
within the genre. Our selections approach the limits of both brevity and
length, ranging from versified jokes to the mock epic *Aloul*.

The social classes represented are about proportional to those in
the whole canon. The concerns for class problems are typical: the
distinctions drawn in *Knights, Clerks, and the Two Churls*; the occasional
indignation against class pride, as in *The Butcher of Abbeville*; and the
frequent depictions of the unsatisfactory marriages which result when
the nobility marry their daughters off to wealthy commoners, as in

---

(Paris: Champion, 1910; repr. New York: Burt Franklin, 1970), and William A. Quinn
and Audley S. Hall, *Jongleur. A Modified Theory of Oral Improvisation and Its Effects
on the Performance and Transmission of Middle English Romances.* (Washington,
D.C. : University Press of America, 1982), especially pp. 1–24.

Berangier of the Long Ass. There are tales of courtly love, tales of common adultery, and tales of common adultery which claim to be courtly (*The Priest Who Peeked, The Wife of Orleans*).

Knights, Clerks, and the Two Churls is the only medieval ecological poem we know of, and we include it for that unique honor. We would like to dedicate it to litterers and those who pave with parking lots the "fair and lovely places" still left in the world.

Fabliaux seldom deal with miracles of life after death. Yet the supernatural tales in this volume couldn't be more diverse. Whereas *Greed and Envy* shocks us into laughing at human depravity, *Saint Peter and the Jongleur* celebrates human frailty in the context of God's love.

Puns, verbal misunderstandings, and physical misunderstandings are much more common plot devices than miracles, although sometimes the faith required to accept them is part of the joke, and the comedy is a product of the stupidity of the misunderstanding and the energy of the response. No sooner have the peasants in *Browny* heard that God returns twofold whatever is given to him, than they are off and running to give away their cow. The same absurd bustle is characteristic of *The Partridges* and *Hearmie* and of many, many fabliaux not translated here.

Confusions over who is alive, who is dead, is another common plot device. While there are many fabliaux of wandering corpses, none are so exhuberant as *The Three Hunchbacks*, and none treat murder and guilt, from the murderers' point of view, with such wit and understanding as *The Sacristan Monk*.

Although the fabliaux are typically stronger in plot than characterization, there are few stories in any genre that integrate character and plot so skillfully as *The Butcher of Abbeville*. The priest's pride compels him to refuse the butcher lodging. Again, it is his pride which later compels him to bully his concubine and his maid. It is his intelligence which allows him to interrogate them successfully and see through their half-truths. It is his pride that suffers most at being fleeced and cuckolded. And it is his intelligence which allows him to articulate his shame, not only at being cuckolded, but at being outwitted: "He wiped my nose on my own sleeve."

Sex is a favorite comic theme, and the treatment of it varies from Henri d'Andeli's, who not only avoids obscene language, but condemns it; through Eustache's and Guerin's use of obscene words at the comic high points of their poems; to the seemingly indiscriminate obscenities of the authors of *The Lady Leech, The Fisherman from Pont-sur-Seine,* and *The Maiden Who Couldn't Hear. . . .* Note, however, that these last three not only use obscene language; they are also *about* language and its power to shock or mask. In each tale the narrator's aggressive use of taboo words contrasts with the euphemisms of one of the characters. Interestingly, one of the most obscene, *The Fisherman . . . ,* is one of the few medieval tales, comic or courtly, which describe sexual compatibility within the sacrament of marriage. *The Maiden* ... , by the way, is the only fabliau plot that the translator remembers as a dirty joke from his childhood, variants having to do with trains and tunnels, cars and garages.

The sense of linguistic propriety which Henry d'Andeli shares with the maiden in the *Maiden Who Couldn't Hear* ... survives, we hope, even into our own more permissive era. Without it, the comic shifts from proper to improper would not work. Unfortunately, this same sense of propriety has often kept the fabliaux from being read at all. But with this volume, we hope to illustrate the versatility of the medieval comic muse.

Appendix

We have used Per Nykrog's siglum classification outlined on pp. 310–11 of his work in order to refer to the various manuscripts in which our fabliaux are located.

Siglum	Name of Manuscript
A	B.N. 837 (anc. 7218)
B	Berne 354
C	Berlin Hamilton 257
D	B.N. 19 152 (anc. St. Germ. 1830)
E	B.N. 1593 (anc. 7615)
F	B.N. 12 603 (anc. suppl. fr. 180)
G	Middleton (Wollaton Hall)
H	B.N. 2168 (anc. 7989)
I	B.N. 25 545 (anc. N.-D. 274)
J	B.N. 1563 (anc. 7595)
K	B.N. 2173 (anc. 7991)
L	B.N. 1635 (anc. 7633)
M	Brit. Mus. Harl. 2253
N	Rome Casanatensis
O	Pavia U.B. 130 E 4
P	B.N. 24 432 (anc. N.-D. 198)
Q	B.N. nouv. acq. 1104
R	Arsenal 3524 (anc. BLF 317)
S	Arsenal 3525 (anc. BLF 318)
T	Chantilly Condé 1578
U	Turin L.V. 32
V	Genève 7 fr. 179
Vbis	Lyon, Bibl. Munic. 5495
W	B.N. 1446 (anc. 7834)
X	B.N. 12581
Y	Brit. Mus. add. 10289
Z	Oxford Digby 86
a	B.N. 375 (anc. 6987)
b	B.N. 1588 (anc. 7609)
c	B.N. 12 483

d	B.N. 14 971
e	Arsenal 3114
f	Chartres 620
g	Rotschild 2800
h	Cambridge Corp. Chr. 50
i	Puy-de-Dôme (fragment)

I. *The Butcher of Abbeville*: MSS *A*, *C*, *H*, *O*, and *T*. We have generally followed *A*. However, as with other translations, where alternate readings seemed better, we have followed them. See Jean Rychner's *Du Bouchier d'Abevile: fabliau du XIIIe siècle,*(Geneva: Droz, 1975), for the texts of all five manuscripts along with his own reading, which generally follows *H* but borrows from the other manuscripts as well. Although we don't always assume with Rychner that the best variant is the earliest and although we disagree with some of his preferences, we do agree that where the manuscripts themselves disagree it is the duty of the translator and the editor to provide the best reading available.

II. *The Tresses*: MSS *B* and *D*. We have chosen *D*.

III. *The Priest Who Peeked*: MSS *E* and *F*. We have used *F*.

IV. *The Wife of Orleans*: This tale (*A*) has two variants: the Berne 354, which contains several mistakes and is somewhat poorer in construction and articulation, and the Hamilton 257 (*C*), which contains some good parts but at times is repetitive and laboriously precise. *C* expands the beating of the husband by twenty-six lines and the farewell scene between wife and lover by twelve lines: neither expansion adds or improves on the tale in any measurable way. Indeed, *C* would gain in being as succinct as *A*: *C*'s husband talks too much, harming the overall effectiveness of some scenes (see Rychner, *Contribution*, 2:84, vv. 76–88, 96–99, and pp. 94, 96, vv. 280–86). On the other hand, *C* (vv. 100–108) describes more carefully the suspicion of the lady, explaining that the pseudo-lover's surprising silence at her greeting has driven her to double-check his identity: *A* could have profited from such a skillful motivation. On the whole, however, *A* is a more representative choice from among the variant versions because of its conciseness, restraint, and emphasis on the action: Paul Theiner calls it a "fine example of a tightly organized, well-constructed fabliau narrative" (CH 127).

V. *Browny, the Priest's Cow*: MS *A*.

VI. *Greed and Envy*: We have used *D* as our text, but this tale is also found in *B*, *C*, and *Vbis*. The last manuscript, called the *Lyon 5495*, contains only two fabliaux and was used as a binding for a Latin codice whose value protected the two tales until they were discovered in 1936. Such are the miracles of survival among fabliaux.

VII. *The Villager and His Two Asses*: MS *D*.

VIII. *Knights, Clerks, and the Two Churls*: MS *A*.

IX. *The Partridges*: MS *A*.

X. *Hearmie*: MS *A*, *B*, and *D*. *A* is the basis for our translation.

XI. *The Fisherman from Pont-Sur-Seine*: MSS *A*, *C*, and *V*. We have used *A*.

XII. *The Lady Leech*: MS *A*.

XIII. *The Maiden Who Couldn't Hear Fuck* ... : of the five versions of this theme, we have chosen *B* for its excellence in construction, character motivation, and style.

XIV. *William of the Falcon*: MS *D*.

XV. *The Lai of Aristotle*: in MSS *A*, *E*, *O*, *D*, and in the Paris Arsenal 3516 (discovered in 1901 and not cited by Nykrog). *D* and the Paris Arsenal manuscript contain several courtly meditations on the power of love not found in the other three. Following the example of Maurice Delbouille (*Le Lai d'Aristote de Henri d'Andeli* [Paris: Les Belles Lettres, 1951]), we have relied principally on *D* and have included these passages as more likely to have been composed by the courtly poet, Henri, than by other fableors or by subsequent jongleurs or scribes.

XVI. *Berangier of the Long Ass*: Guerin's tale, from MS *D*, has been preferred over its anonymous version in *A* for the tight structuring of its narrative, its artful descriptions of the husband's excursions, its stronger motivations, and its theme of class conflict, which adds a new dimension to the eternal theme of domestic conflict and domination.

XVII. *Aloul*: MS *A*.

XVIII. *Saint Peter and the Jongleur*: in two MSS, *A* and *D*. Our translation is from *A*, except for the reckoning of the stakes, from *D*. The betting is incomprehensible in *A*, but can be understood in *D* once we realize that the initial three souls, which evidently stay in the pot, are sometimes counted as part of the winning, sometimes not.

XIX. *The Three Hunchbacks*: MS *A*.

XX. *The Sacristan Monk*: MSS *B*, *C*, *D*, and *d*. We have used *D*.

BIBLIOGRAPHY

I. Editions

Delbouille, Maurice. *Le Lai d'Aristote de Henri d'Andeli*. Paris: Société d'Edition "Les Belles Lettres," 1951.

Johnston, R. C., and D. D. R. Owen. *Fabliaux*. Oxford: Basil Blackwell, 1957.

Levy, B. J. *Selected Fabliaux, Edited from the B.N. Fonds Français 837 Fonds Français 19152 and Berlin Hamilton 257*. University of Hull: Department of French, 1978.

Livingston, Charles H. *Le Jongleur Gautier le Leu: Etude sur les fabliaux*. Cambridge, Mass.: Harvard University Press, 1951.

Montaiglon, Anatole de, and Gaston Raynaud. *Recueil général et complet des fabliaux des XIIIe et XIVe siècles*. 6 vols. Paris: Librairie des Bibliophiles, 1872–90; repr. New York: Burt Franklin, n.d.; repr. Geneva: Slatkine, 1973.

Noomen, Willem, and Nico van den Boogaard. *Nouveau recueil complet des fabliaux*. 4 vols. Assen: Van Gorcum, 1983–84.

O'Gorman, Richard. *"Les Braies au cordelier": Anonymous Fabliau of the Thirteenth Century*. Birmingham, Ala.: Summa Publications, 1983.

Reid, T. B. W. *Twelve Fabliaux*. Manchester: Manchester University Press, 1968.

Rychner, Jean. *Du Bouchier d'Abevile: Fabliau du XIIIe siècle (Eustache d'Amiens)*. Geneva: Droz, 1975.

II. Translations

Benson, Larry D., and Theodore M. Andersson, eds. and trans. *The Literary Context of Chaucer's Fabliaux*. Indianapolis and New York: The Bobbs-Merrill Co., Inc., 1971.

Brians, Paul. *Bawdy Tales from the Courts of Medieval France*. New York: Harper and Row, 1972.

DuVal, John. "The Villager and His Two Asses." In *Intro 7*, ed. George Garrett, 273–75. Garden City, N.Y.: Doubleday Anchor Books, 1975.

——. "Les Tresces: Semi-Tragical Fabliau, Critique and Translation." *Publications of the Missouri Philological Association* 3 (1979): 7-16.

——. "Medieval French Fabliaux." *Lazarus* 1 (1980): 8-49.

Eichmann, Raymond, ed., and John DuVal, trans. *Cuckolds, Clerics and Countrymen. Medieval French Fabliaux.* Fayetteville: University of Arkansas Press, 1982.

——. *The French Fabliau: The Ms. B.N. 837.* Vol. 1. New York: Garland Publishing Inc., 1983.

——. *The French Fabliau: The Ms. B.N. 837.* Vol. 2. New York: Garland Publishing Inc., l985.

Harrison, Robert. *Gallic Salt.* Berkeley: University of California Press, 1974.

Hellman, Robert, and Richard O'Gorman. *Fabliaux: Ribald Tales from the Old French.* New York: Crowell, 1965.

Orr, John, ed. and trans. *Eustache d'Amiens: "Le Boucher d'Abbeville."* London: Oliver and Boyd, 1947.

Rickard, Peter et al. *Medieval Comic Tales.* Totowa, New Jersey: Rowman and Littlefield, 1973.

III. Critical Works

Akehurst, F. R. P. "Cognitive Orientations in the Fabliaux: Contribution to a Study of the Audiences of Thirteenth-Century French Literature." *Reading Medieval Studies* 9 (1983): 45-55.

Beach, Charles Ray. *Treatment of Ecclesiastics in the French Fabliaux of the Middle Ages.* Modern Language Series, 34. Lexington: University Press of Kentucky, 1960.

Bédier, Joseph. *Les Fabliaux.* 6th ed. Paris: Champion, 1964.

Bloch, R. Howard. "The Fabliaux, Fetishism, and Freud's Jewish Jokes." *Representations* 4 (1983): 1-26.

——. *The Scandal of the Fabliaux.* Chicago: University of Chicago Press, 1986.

Brewer, D. S. "The Fabliaux." In *Companion to Chaucer Studies,* ed. Beryl Rowland, 247-67. New York: Oxford University Press, 1968.

Busby, Keith. "Courtly Literature and the Fabliaux: Some Instances of Parody." Section 131, International Congress on Medieval Studies, Kalamazoo, Michigan, May 1982.

——. "Courtly Literature and the Fabliaux: Some Instances of Parody." *Zeitschrift für Romanische Philologie* 102 (1986): 67-87.

Canby, Henry S. "The English Fabliau." *Publications of the Modern Language Association* 21 (1906): 200-214.

Cooke, Thomas D. "Formulaic Diction and the Artistry of 'Le Chevalier qui recovra l'Amor de sa Dame.'" *Romania* 94 (1973): 232-40.

——. "Pornography, the Comic Spirit, and the Fabliaux." In *The Humor of the Fabliaux: A Collection of Critical Essays,* ed. Thomas D. Cooke and Benjamin L. Honeycutt, 137–62. Columbia: University of Missouri Press, 1974.

———. *The Old French and Chaucerian Fabliaux: A Study of Their Comic Climax.* Columbia: University of Missouri Press, 1978.

Cooke, Thomas D., and Benjamin L. Honeycutt, eds. *The Humor of the Fabliaux: A Collection of Critical Essays.* Columbia: University of Missouri Press, 1974.

Dronke, Peter. "The Rise of the Medieval Fabliau: Latin and Vernacular Evidence." *Romanische Forschungen* 85 (1973): 275–97.

Eichmann, Raymond. "The Question of Variants and the Fabliaux." *Fabula* 17 (1976): 40–44.

———. "The Search for Originals in the Fabliaux and the Validity of Textual Dependency." *Romance Notes* 19 (1978): 90–97.

———. "The Anti-Feminism of the Fabliaux." *French Literature Series: Authors and Philosophers*, vol. 6, ed. A. Maynor Hardee, 26–34. Columbia S.C.: University of South Carolina, 1979.

———. "Oral Composition: A Recapitulatory View of its Value and Impact." *Neuphilologische Mitteilungen* 80 (1979): 97–109.

———. "The Artistry of Economy in the Fabliaux." *Studies in Short Fiction* 17 (1980): 67–73.

———. "The 'Her(m)ites' of the 'Bouchier d'Abeville.'" *South Central Review* 2, no. 4 (Winter 1985): 1–8.

———. "The Failure of Literary Language in 'Guillaume au Faucon.'" In *Reinardus*. Yearbook of the International Reynard Society, vol. 1, ed. Brian Levy and Paul Wackers, 72–78. Grave: Alfa, 1988.

Faral, Edmond. *Les Jongleurs en France au moyen âge.* Paris: Champion, 1910; repr. New York: Burt Franklin, 1970.

———. "Le Fabliau latin au moyen âge." *Romania* 50 (1924): 321–85.

Flutre, Louis-Fernand. "Le Fabliau, genre courtois?" *Frankfurter Universitätsreden* 22 (1960): 70–84.

Hart, Walter Morris. "The Fabliau and Popular Literature." *Publications of the Modern Language Association* 23 (1908): 329–74.

———. "The Narrative Art of the Old French Fabliau." In *Anniversary Papers by Colleagues and Pupils of George Lyman Kittredge*, 209–16. Boston: Ginn and Company, 1913.

Helsinger, Howard. "Pearls in the Swill: Comic Allegory in the French Fabliaux." In *The Humor of the Fabliaux: A Collection of Critical Essays*, ed. Thomas D. Cooke and Benjamin L. Honeycutt, 93–105. Columbia: University of Missouri Press, 1974.

Henry, Charles. "The Grip of Winter in 'Des Trois Bossus,' an Old French Fabliau." *Comparative Literature Studies* 6 (1979): 26–34.

Holmes, Urban T. "Notes on the French Fabliau." In *Middle Ages, Reformation, Volkskunde: Festschrift for John G. Kunstmann*, 39–44. Chapel Hill: University of North Carolina Press, 1959.

Honeycutt, Benjamin L. "The Knight and His World as Instruments of

Humor in the Fabliaux." In *The Humor of the Fabliaux: A Collection of Critical Essays*, ed. Thomas D. Cooke and Benjamin L. Honeycutt, 75-92. Columbia: University of Missouri Press, 1974.

———. "An Example of Comic Cliché in the Old French Fabliaux." *Romania* 96 (1975): 245-55.

Johnson, Lesley. "Women on Top: Antifeminism in the Fabliaux." *Modern Language Review* 78, no. 2 (1983): 298-307.

Kasprzyk, Krystyna. "Pour la sociologie du fabliau: Convention, tactique et engagement." *Kwartalnik Neofilologiczny* 23 (1976): 153-61.

Lacy, Gregg F. "Augustinian Imagery and Fabliau 'Obscenity.'" In *Studies on the Seven Sages of Rome and Other Essays in Medieval Literature: Dedicated to the Memory of Jean Misrahi*, ed. Henri Niedzielski et al., 219-30. Honolulu: Educational Research Associates, 1978.

———. "Fabliau Stylistic Humor." *Kentucky Romance Quarterly* 26 (1979): 349-59.

Lacy, Norris J. "Types of Esthetic Distance in the Fabliaux." In *The Humor of the Fabliaux: A Collection of Critical Essays*, ed. Thomas D. Cooke and Benjamin L. Honeycutt, 107-17. Columbia: University of Missouri Press, 1974.

———. "The Fabliaux and Comic Logic." *Esprit Créateur* 16 (1976): 39-45.

———. "Fabliau Women." *Romance Notes* 25 (1985): 318-27.

Ladd, A. "Classification of the Fabliaux by Plot Structure." In *University of Glasgow, International Beast Epic Colloquium, 23-25 September 1975*, ed. K. Varty, 92-107. Glasgow: n.p., 1976.

Levy, Brian, and Paul Wackers, eds. *Reinardus*. Yearbook of the International Reynard Society. 2 vols. Grave: Alfa, 1988, 1989.

Lian, A. P. "Aspects of Verbal Humour in the Old French Fabliaux." In *Australasian Universities Language and Literature Association: Proceedings and Papers at the Twelfth Congress*, 235-61. Sydney: AULLA, 1970.

Livingston, Charles H. "Le jongleur Gautier Le Leu. A Study in the Fabliaux." *Romanic Review* 15 (1924): 1-67.

———. "The Fabliau 'Des Deux Anglois et de l'anel.'" *Publications of the Modern Language Association* 40 (1925): 217-24.

Lorcin, Marie-Thérèse. *Façons de sentir et de penser: les fabliaux français*. Paris: Champion, 1979.

Ménard, Philippe. *Les Fabliaux, contes à rire du moyen âge*. Paris: PUF, 1979.

Muscatine, Charles. *Chaucer and the French Tradition*. Berkeley: University of California Press, 1957.

———. "The Wife of Bath and Gautier's 'La Veuve.'" In *Romance Studies in Memory of Edward Bilings Ham*, ed. Urban T. Holmes, 109-14. Hayward, California: California State College, 1967.

——. "The Social Background of the Old French Fabliaux." *Genre* 9 (1976): 1–19.

——. *The Old French Fabliaux.* New Haven: Yale University Press, 1986.

Noomen, Willem. "Qu'est-ce qu'un fabliau?" In *XIV Congresso di Linguistica e Filologia Romanza: Acti V*, ed. Alberto Vàrvaro, 431–32. Naples: Macchiaroli, 1981; Amsterdam: Benjamins, 1981.

Nykrog, Per. *Les Fabliaux: Etude d'histoire littéraire et de stylistique médiévale.* Copenhagen: Ejnar Munksgaard, 1957; repr. with Postscript, Geneva: Droz, 1973.

——. "Courtliness and the Townspeople: The Fabliaux as a Courtly Burlesque." In *The Humor of the Fabliaux: A Collection of Critical Essays*, ed. Thomas D. Cooke and Benjamin L. Honeycutt, 59–73. Columbia: University of Missouri Press, 1974.

Olson, Glending. "'The Reeve's Tale' and 'Gombert.'" *Modern Language Review* 64 (1969): 721–25.

——. "The Medieval Theory of Literature for Refreshment and Its Use in the Fabliau Tradition." *Studies in Philology* 71 (1974): 291–313.

——. "'The Reeve's Tale' as a Fabliau." *Modern Language Quarterly* 35 (1974): 219–30.

Owen, D. D. R. "The Element of Parody in 'Saint Pierre et le Jongleur.'" *French Studies* 9 (1955): 60–63.

Patzer, Otto. "The Wealth of the Clergy in the Fabliaux." *Modern Language Notes* 19 (1904): 195–96.

Pearcy, Roy J. "A Minor Analogue to the Branding in 'The Miller's Tale.'" *Notes and Queries* 16 (1969): 333–35.

——. "A Classical Analogue to 'Le Preudome qui rescolt son compere de noier.'" *Romance Notes* 12 (1971): 422–27.

——. "Realism and Religious Parody in the Fabliaux: Watriquet de Couvin's 'Les Trois Dames de Paris.'" *Revue belge de philologie et d'histoire* 50 (1972): 744–54.

——. "Relations between the D and A Versions of 'Berengier au long Cul.'" *Romance Notes* 14 (1972): 1–6.

——. "'Le Prestre qui menga les meures' and Ovid's 'Fasti, III, 745–760.'" *Romance Notes* 15 (1973): 159–63.

——. "Modes of Signification and the Humor of Obscene Diction in the Fabliaux." In *The Humor of the Fabliaux: A Collection of Critical Essays*, ed. Thomas D. Cook and Benjamin L. Honeycutt, 163–69. Columbia: University of Missouri Press, 1974.

——. "Structural Models for the Fabliaux and the Summoner's Tale's Analogues." *Fabula* 13 (1974): 103–13.

——. "An Instance of Heroic Parody in the Fabliaux." *Romania* 98 (1977): 105–7.

——. "Investigations into the Principles of Fabliau Structure." In *Versions of Medieval Comedy*, ed. Paul Ruggiers, 67–100. Norman: University of Oklahoma Press, 1977.

——. "Chansons de geste and Fabliaux: 'La Gageure' and 'Berenger au long cul.'" *Neuphilologische Mitteilungen* 79 (1978): 76–83.

Pitts, Brent A. "Truth-Seeking Discourse in the Old French Fabliaux." *Medievalia et Humanistica* 15 (1985): 95–117.

——. "Merveilleux, Mirage and Comic Ambiguity in the Old French Fabliaux." *Assays* 4 (1987): 39–50.

Robbins, Rossell Hope. "The English Fabliau: Before and After Chaucer." *Moderna Sprak* 64 (1970): 231–44.

Rowland, Beryl. "What Chaucer Did to the Fabliaux." *Studia Neophilologica* 51 (1979): 205–13.

Rychner, Jean. *Contribution à l'étude des fabliaux: Variantes, remaniements, dégradations.* 2 vols. Geneva: Droz; Paris: Minard, 1960.

——. "Les Fabliaux: genre, styles, publics." In *La Littérature narrative d'imagination.* Edited by Faculté des Lettres de l'Université de Strasbourg, 41–54. Paris: Presses Universitaires de France, 1961.

Schaar, Claes. "The Merchant's Tale," "Amadas et Ydoine," and "Guillaume au Faucon." *Bulletin de la soc. royale des lettres de Lund* 2 (1952–53): 87–95.

Schenck, Mary Jane Stearns. "The Morphology of the Fabliau." *Fabula* 17 (1976): 26–39.

——. "Functions and Roles in the Fabliaux." *Comparative Literature* 30 (1978): 22–24.

——. "Les Structures narratives dans le 'Cuvier.'" *Marche Romane* 28 (1978): 185–92.

——. "Narrative Structure in the Exemplum, Fabliau, and the Nouvelle." *Romanic Review* 72 (1981): 367–82.

——. *The Fabliaux. Tales of Wit and Deception.* Purdue University Monographs in Romance Languages, vol. 24. Amsterdam and Philadelphia: John Benjamins, 1987.

Stillwell, Gardiner. "The Language of Love in Chaucer's Miller's and Reeve's Tales and in the Old French Fabliaux." *Journal of English and Germanic Philology* 44 (1955): 693–99.

Subrenat, Jean. "Notes sur la tonalité des fabliaux. A propos du fabliau 'Du Fèvre de Creeil.'" *Marche Romane* 25 (1975): 83–93.

Taylor, Steven M. "Folk Wisdom and the Fabliaux: Rhetorical and Risible Uses of Proverbs." *Michigan Academician* 16 (1984): 237–51.

Theiner, Paul. "Fabliau Settings." In *The Humor of the Fabliaux: A Collection of Critical Essays,* ed. Thomas D. Cooke and Benjamin L. Honeycutt, 119–36. Columbia: University of Missouri Press, 1974.

Togeby, Knud. "The Nature of the Fabliaux." In *The Humor of the Fabliaux: A Collection of Critical Essays,* ed. Thomas D. Cooke and Benjamin L. Honeycutt, 7–13. Columbia: University of Missouri Press, 1974.

Varty, Kenneth, ed. *University of Glasgow, International Beast Epic Colloquium, 23-25 September 1975.* Glasgow: n.p., 1976.

Wailes, Stephen L. "The Unity of the Fabliau 'Un Chivalier et sa dame et un clerk.'" *Romance Notes* 14 (1972): 593-96.

———. "Vagantes and the Fabliaux." In *The Humor of the Fabliaux: A Collection of Critical Essays,* ed. Thomas D. Cooke and Benjamin L. Honeycutt, 43-58. Columbia: University of Missouri Press, 1974.

———. "Role-Playing in Medieval *Comediae* and Fabliaux." *Neuphilologische Mitteilungen* 75 (1974): 640-49.

White, Sarah Melhado. "Sexual Language and Human Conflict in Old French Fabliaux." *Comparative Studies in Society and History* 24 (1982): 185-210.

Williams, Harry F. "French Fabliau Scholarship." *South Atlantic Review* 46 (1981): 76-82.

Fabliaux, Fair and Foul

I *The Butcher of Abbeville*

EUSTACHE D'AMIENS

Eustache d'Amiens' only known work is perhaps the most admired of the medieval French fabliaux. The five extant manuscripts of the poem attest to its popularity in Eustache's day. In our time, as recently as 1975, Jean Rychner has reaffirmed the poem's worth by publishing all five manuscript versions, along with his own edited version, in a single book. Roy J. Pearcy praises Eustache as a "polished artist" whose lone work is to be admired for "tightness of . . . plot, . . . excellent character portrayal, enhanced by lively dialogue" (CH 186).

> Listen, my lords, to what I say.[1]
> Never have you, until today,
> Heard such a wonder as I shall tell.
> Gather around and listen well.
> You know, my lords, that any word
> Is wasted when it isn't heard.
> A butcher lived in Abbeville
> Whose neighbors bore him much good will.
> He wasn't evil-tongued or cold,
> But wise, well-mannered, courteous, bold,
> Dedicated to his trade,
> Considerate and quick to aid
> His neighbors who were poor and needy.
> He wasn't miserly or greedy.
> Near All Saints' Day this butcher went
> To the marketplace at Oisement
> To buy livestock. It wasn't long
> Before he wished he hadn't gone.
> The animals were far from cheap.
> The goats were scrawny, so were the sheep.
> The pigs were low grade, tough and poor,
> Not worth his while to bargain for.

10 (line 10 marker)
20 (line 20 marker)

---

[1] For the description of the manuscripts of this and the other tales, see appendix.

His time was wasted. He had spent
Most of the day, and not a cent.
　　Now that the day was almost gone,
He threw his outer jacket on
Above his sword and left at last
From Oisement market, walking fast.
Now hear what happened. Evening fell
30   As he was going through Balluel,
Just halfway home from where he'd been.
He thought he'd have to find an inn
And put up there until the dawn.
Now that the dark was coming on,
He feared that robbers might attack
Him on the road and take his sack,
Which still was full. He saw a poor
Woman standing by her door
And asked her, "Ma'am, could you suggest
40   A place to sleep. I need some rest.
I'll gladly pay. I think it's better
Not to be someone else's debtor."
The woman courteously replied,
"By God, who for us sinners died,
According to my husband, Giles,
The only wine around for miles
Is what belongs to our parish priest.
He brought two vats of it at least
From Nogentel a week ago.
50   In my opinion you should go
To the rectory for board and bed."
—"I'll go there now," the butcher said,
"May God in heaven be with you."
—"Faith, sir," she said, "God bless you too."
　　This parish priest, puffed up with pride,
Was sitting on the step outside.
The butcher said, "God grant you grace.
For the love of God, give me a place
To sleep tonight, and for your trouble,
60   God will reward you more than double."
The priest replied, "*God* lodge you then,
For by the saints and holy men,
The laity may not lie here.
You'll find a good room fairly near
Somewhere or other in the town.
Go search the village up and down
Till you find lodgings, and sleep there,

Not on my premises; I swear
I'll never let you come inside.
70   What's more, the rooms are occupied.
For priests to have to entertain
Common folk goes against my grain."
—"Common, sir! Do you mean to be
Contemptuous of the laity?"
—"Indeed I do, boy, and why not?
Enough of this. Get off my lot.
This strikes me as impertinence."
—"No, sir, but it's beneficence
To let me sleep here. You must know
80   There's nowhere else for me to go.
I don't mind spending what is mine.
If you should like to sell some wine,
You'll have my lasting gratitude.
I'll pay you though: my money's good.
It wouldn't cost anything."
—"You might as well be battering
This heavy rock against your head,
For by St. Peter," the priest said,
"In my abode you'll never sleep."
90   The butcher said, "The devil keep
Your house, vile priest. To Hell with you—
Frivolous fool, and common, too!"
At that he left. What more to say?
Heart full of wrath he stormed away.
Now hear what happened. During the night
Just outside town the butcher caught sight
Of an old dilapidated building
Whose roof had half caved in—and milling
Around the walls were lambs and sheep.
100   The shepherd was one who used to keep
Large herds of cattle in his day.
"Shepherd," he asked, "whose sheep are they?"
—"Good sir, the priest owns all of them."
—"Is that so?" said the butcher, "Hmmm."
    Listen to what the butcher did:
Protected by the night, he hid
A sheep so slyly in his coat
That the old shepherd took no note.
Once out of sight, he shouldered the load
110   And went back by another road
To where the crude and haughty pastor
Was shutting his door. "May the great Master

And Judge of men be good to you,"
Said the man with the sheep, "how do you do?"
The priest replied, "Where'd you come from?"
—"From Abbeville, but I've just come
From Oisement Market where I sought
Some high-grade meat. All that I bought
Was this one sheep, but what a buy!
120   He's heavy in the flank and thigh.
If you would let me lodge here, please,
For your advantage and your ease,
I promise you, I won't be cheap:
Tonight we will enjoy this sheep
For dinner, sir, if you agree.
Its weight has been too much for me.
He's got enough fat, tender meat
For everyone in the house to eat."
        Deceived, the priest, who never rued
130   Eating someone else's food
And who liked one thing that was dead
Better than four still living, said,
"Yes, willingly, I do agree.
You're welcome here. If there were three
Of you, my house would be sufficient.
Never have I been found deficient
In courtesy or honest dealing.
You're a gentleman, I have a feeling.
Tell me, I pray, what is your name?"
140   —"David, in truth. The name's the same
As I received it in baptism
From parish priest with oil and chrism.
This trip's been hard," he told the priest;
"May he who owned this heavy beast
Never see the light of Heaven.
And now let's put him in the oven."
        This time the butcher was invited
Into the house. A fire was lighted.
The butcher put his burden down,
150   Took a hasty look around,
And told the parson that he ought
To have an ax, so one was brought.
He killed the sheep and dressed it, too.
The thick and heavy fleece he threw
Across a beam before their eyes.
"Come here," he said, "Sir, what a prize
This sheep is! Will you take a look!

There's grade-A mutton on the hook.
This fellow grew up big and stout—
160   Too big, in fact, for I'm worn out
From having to carry him for hours.
Do with him what you like. He's yours.
Roast the shoulders. Put the rest
Into a kettle for the best
Lamb stew your household ever ate.
All other meat is second rate.
There's never been more tender flesh.
Look how it's succulent and fresh.
Just put it on the flames to heat.
170   It will be done enough to eat
Before you can prepare the sauce."
—"Good guest, you do it. I'm at a loss.
Compared with you, I am unable
To manage this." —"Then set the table."
—"It's set. I'll have the candles lit.
Let's wash. We'll eat when you see fit."
    I can no longer, lords, ignore
The presence of a paramour
For whom the priest was so possessed
180   By jealousy that when a guest
Would visit, he would make her stay
Inside her room; but on that day
At his command the lady joined
Them at the table. He made a point
Of treating her with great affection.
When they had dined to their satisfaction,
The lady had her servants spread
Some fresh white sheets on her guest's bed.
The pastor called the maid, "My dear,
190   Attend to our guest while he is here.
Make sure Sir David takes delight
In everything done for him tonight.
Do nothing counter to his whim,
Since we have profited by him."
They went to bed together then,
The lady and the priest, I mean;
The butcher rested by the fire.
There wasn't a thing he could desire.
He had a roof and a warm bed.
200   "Come over here, my dear," he said
To the servant girl; "Let's talk this over.
Kindly let me be your lover.

I promise you you'll profit by it."
—"Good guest! What folly, please be quiet!
That's the worst thing I ever heard."
—"You'll do it, though. You can't afford
To refuse an offer such as this."
—"All right. Tell me what it is."
—"If you would do my will tonight
210   And do my joy and my delight,
As God's my witness, you may keep
The fleece I stripped from off my sheep."
—"Now don't go saying that to me.
You're not a holy hermit, I see,
Coming here with this request.
You certainly are a naughty guest.
Glory to God, what a fool you are.
I'd do your will, but I don't dare.
You'd tell my mistress all tomorrow."
220   —"May God condemn my soul to sorrow
If ever I give a hint or clue
Of this affair or tell on you."
The maid believed in what he said,
And so she did his will in bed
All night until the night was done
Then got up with the rising sun,
Built up the fire and fed the beasts.
        Soon afterward arose the priest,
Who went together with his clerk
230   To church to sing and do their work.
The lady stayed in bed and slept.
Her guest, however, straightaway leapt
From bed, put on his shoes and dressed.
Time to be up; no time to rest.
He went upstairs to bid farewell
Now to the parson's demoiselle.[1]
He quietly undid the lock
And opened the door. The lady woke,
Opened her eyes, turned her head,
240   And saw him standing by her bed.
She asked where he had come from, sir!
What did he have to do with her?
"My lady, thanks" he said, "Last night
I lodged with you to my delight."

---

[1] Demoiselle: young unmarried woman.

He moved toward the pillow, stood above her,
And gently pulled away the cover,
And there she lay. The lady's guest
Beheld her snow-white throat and breast.
"What miracle do my eyes feast
250   Upon? St. Romalcus! This priest[1]
Leads a charmed life—and Lord! what charms—
Naked in such a lady's arms!
St. Honoré salvation bring!
She would do honor to a king.
I wish to God someone would let
Me lie a little here and get
Refreshment, comfort, ease from pain!"
—"Oh, no!" she answered him, "it's plain
You don't ask much. Sir! I command
260   You leave this room. Remove your hand!
The pastor's singing should be done.
He'll think there's something going on!
If he should find me with a man,
He'll never care for me again.
You'll be the death of me for sure."
The butcher calmed her down and swore,
"Lady, by Mary full of grace,
I am not moving from this place,
Not for any man alive,
270   Not if the pastor should arrive,
For if he did, and said one word
That was outrageous or absurd,
I'd kill the man. Now hear my offer:
If you consent to be my lover
And do my will, then you'll receive
My wooly sheepskin when I leave.
It's worth more money than I could pay."
—"I wouldn't dare! What would people say?
I think you're mad. You wouldn't lose
280   A minute before you spread the news."
—"Lady," he said, "you must have faith.
As long as I have life and breath,
By all the Saints in Rome I swear
I'll tell nobody anywhere."
The butcher urged and pled until
The lady yielded to his will,

---

[1] St. Romalcus: 7th century Bishop of Maastricht, Holland.

And for the sheepskin he would owe her
She put her body in his power,
Which the butcher took advantage of.
290   And after he had had enough,
He left. He had no need for staying.
He went to church. The priest was praying
The lesson with his acolyte.
The butcher didn't hesitate.
Just as he said *Jube Domne*[1]
He came into the church. "Good day,"
He told the priest, "last night you lodged
Me comfortably. I'm much obliged.
Your hospitality is the best.
300   However, I have one request.
This is the last of my demands.
Please take my sheepskin off my hands
And make my journey light today.
Three pounds the wool alone must weigh.
It's a good fleece, I promise you.
It's worth three sous. Take it for two.
I'd be most grateful if you'd have it."
—"I will indeed, for your sake, David,
Most willingly for love of you.
310   You're a good friend, loyal and true.
Come back as often as you please."
The butcher sold the priest's own fleece
Then said good-bye and off he went.
        The lady, who was elegant
And beautiful, arose and dressed
In a green gown that had been pressed
In neatly folded pleats. She laced
It very tightly at the waist
To satisfy her vanity.
320   She was as pleasing as could be.
Her eyes were lively, bright, and clear.
She came and sat down in a chair.
Just then the serving girl came in
And was about to take the skin,
When the lady stopped her: "Wait, my girl.
Inform me please, who in the world

---

[1] The acolyte addresses the priest: "*Jube Domne, benedicare*" (Pray, father, a blessing). Helsinger remarks that "the butcher's offer is a markedly ironic response to the prayer" (CH 102).

Told you to take that fleece from there?"
—"Madam, this fleece is my affair.
It's too much in the way inside.
330   I'll leave it out until it's dried,
Hanging in the sun and air."
—"Well don't," she said, "Just leave it there.
Go do the work you're paid to do."
—"Ma'am, I rose earlier than you
And did my work, though I admit
I haven't had much thanks for it.
You shouldn't mention work to me."
—"Get out, and let the sheepskin be.
Just keep your fingers off the hide.
340   Don't meddle with it." —The maid replied,
"I will, by God, in spite of you.
I'll meddle with this skin. I'll do
What I want with what belongs to me."
—"You think the skin is yours, I see?"
—"That's what I think and what I know."
—"Well put it down!" said the lady; "Go!
Get out. Go hang yourself or drown
In the outhouse hole. And don't you frown
At me. You've gotten much too big
350   For your own britches, hussy! Pig!
You leave my house at once. Get out!"
—"But ma'am, abusing me about
What's mine is foolish. You may swear
By all the saints that ever were—
The skin's still mine." —"In any case
Get out of my sight. Go drown some place.
Your service is no longer needed.
You've bungled here too long—and cheated.
Whatever my lord may have decreed
360   Your job here isn't guaranteed.
Today you've earned my lasting hate."
—"Plague take the woman who would wait
On you again. I'll stay until
The master comes, and then I'll tell
On you and tell what's going on,
And after that, good-bye, I'm gone."
—"Is that right, now? You'll tell the master?
You stinking slut, whore, pig, bitch, bastard!"
—"Bastard? Ma'am! Come now, admit
370   Exactly how legitimate
Your children by the priest have been."

—"By God's passion! Drop that skin!
Keep it, and it will cost you dear!
You'll wish you were in Arras, not here,
Cologne, by God, or Switzerland."
She took the distaff in her hand
And struck the girl. The girl exclaimed,
"By Mary Queen of Heaven, shame!
Oh what a woeful blow you've dealt!
380   Believe me though, you'll buy this pelt
At a high price before I die!"
She started to weep and wail and cry.
        The priest, who heard the noise and fuss,
Came in to see what the matter was.
—"What's going on? Who dared assault you?"
—"The mistress, sir. She had no call to."
—"Without some call, I'm sure your lady
Wouldn't have beaten you so badly."
—"Sir, she did it for that hide
390   That's hanging by the fireside.
Last night before you went to bed
You gave me orders, sir, and said
I should give comfort to our guest,
Sir David, just as he thought best.
I did just as you ordered, sir.
He gave the skin to me, not her.
May my immortal soul be burned
If it's not mine. It's what I earned!"
The priest concluded that the maid
400   Had earned the skin by getting laid;
Despite his wrath he didn't dare
Accuse her of it then and there.
"Lady," he said, "I clearly see
You haven't been doing right by me.
Beat my servant, and you neglect
To offer me my due respect."
—"Bah! She wanted my fleece. My Lord,
It served her right. If you had heard
The way she kept insulting me,
410   You'd tell me I did well. Why she
Insinuates that I bear shame
For your own children. You're to blame.
You keep on letting her besmatter
My reputation with her chatter.
She may dispute the fact for years,
But *my* fleece never will be hers."

—"Your fleece?" —"Yes!" —"May I ask why?"
—"Your guest in my house slept on my
Clean sheets last night and on my cot,
420   By St. Acheus, if you've got[1]
To question all I say to you."
—"My lady, come now, tell me true,
By the faith you promised me and swore
When first you entered through this door:
This fleece, should it indeed be yours?"
—"Yes! By all the saints, of course!"
The servant girl broke in: "My Lord,
Don't you believe a word you've heard.
The skin was given me before
430   It was to her." —"Damn you, you whore,
Hot pants is all that you were given.
Get out of my house before you're driven,
And may misfortune be your guide."
—"Now by the cross," the priest replied,
"Lady, I say you're in the wrong."
—"Oh no, I'm not. My anger's strong
Enough to kill the girl. In brief,
I hate the lying little thief."
—"What have I ever stolen, ma'am?"
440   —"Slut! My barley, peas and ham—
She steals my fresh baked bread, my flour—
Why you continue to allow her
To make her home here I don't know.
Pay her wages, let her go,
And be well rid of her at last."
—"Lady," he answered, "not so fast.
What I still want to know is this:
Whose property the sheepskin is,
And if it's yours, then say who gave it."
450   —"Our guest did when he left, Sir David."
—"Now by the holy eucharist cup,
This guest you talk about was up
And gone before the break of day.
There's no believing what you say,
The way you swear to God and lie."
—"But he politely said good-bye
Before he left," the lady said.
—"While you were getting out of bed?"

---

[1] St. Acheus: martyred at Amiens, 302 AD.

—"No." —"Well, when?" —"While I was still
Asleep. I didn't notice till
He stood beside my pillow. I mean,
My Lord, I think I should explain—"
—"Exactly how did he say goodbye?"
—"Sir! Are you trying to imply . . .
All he said was, 'Peace of the Lord!'
And left without another word,
Not a request, not a suggestion,
Nothing was done. There was no question
Of any blemish or affront
To your good name, but you must hunt
For ruses to accuse me of.
You're never satisfied. You love
To hunt deceit, but find in me
Nothing, thank God, but honesty.
You've kept me in this house imprisoned
Until my flesh is pale and wizened.
You've closed me up inside a cage
To molt and wilt until old age.
I've let my nature be subdued
By you too long for drink and food."
—"Too long indeed, ungrateful cheat,
I've let you take your ease and eat!
You've got a beating coming to you!
I know the truth. You let him screw you!
Why didn't you scream? This time we're through.
I'm going to have to break with you.
Out of my house! Go! Leave it now!
I'm going to my church to vow
Upon the bones of the holy dead
Never again to share your bed!"
Infuriated, filled with grief,
He sat down, shaking like a leaf.
The lady realized that the pastor
Wouldn't hear reason. He was mastered
By rage. She wished that she'd kept silence.
Fearing that he might do her violence,
She turned and went back to her chamber.
    The shepherd, who had found the number
Of sheep he had was short by one,
Came to the house at a terrible run,
Not knowing where it could have been.
He reached the door and tramped on in,
Looking in corners everywhere.

The priest was sitting in his chair,
Simmering with indignation.
"What's this? What's going on? Damnation
Take your soul. Where'd you come from?
Where are your sheep, you no-good bum?
Son of a bitch! You're playing some trick.
510   I ought to beat you with my stick.
You should be tending to your herd."
—"Sir! One of the sheep has disappeared,
The prize of all your flock, the chief!
He's gone, and I can't find the thief."
—"I understand. You've lost a sheep.
You're paid to guard them, not to sleep!
A hanging's what you ought to get."
—"Listen, sir. Last night I met
A man I never chanced to meet
520   In town, in fields, or on the street
Until just then. I saw him look
Long and hard, sir, at my flock.
He asked whose sheep they were. Of course
I answered, sir, that they were yours.
It's him who stole it, I suggest."
—"By God, that must have been our guest,
David. Here's where he spent the night.
He made a fool of me all right,
Screwed everyone in the rectory
530   And sold my own damn skin to me.
He wiped my nose with my own sleeve.
I'm born to be deceived and grieve,
Letting that trickster get away....
Well, live and learn from day to day.
He rolled me out in my own dough!
Is this your sheep's pelt, would you know?"
—"Yes, sir," the shepherd told the priest,
"I'd recognize my own sheep's fleece.
For seven years I've been its master."
540   He took the sheepskin from the pastor,
Examined head and ears and chin
And knew it was his own sheep's skin.
—"Alas the day that I was born, he
Is the one, sir. That's old Horny,
The animal I loved the best,
The finest, fattest, wooliest.
By good St. Vincent, sir, there wasn't
A better sheep among ten dozen.

A better couldn't have been at all."
550   —"Come here, my Lady," the pastor called,
"And answer me as I command.
And you, my girl, come here and stand
And answer when I tell you to.
You claim this skin belongs to you?"
—"Yes, sir, as I'm a loyal maid,
I claim it all," the servant said.
—"Fair Lady, you, whose shall it be?"
—"By God, that skin belongs to me.
It should be mine and mine alone."
560   —"It won't be either's. It's my own,
Bought with my money. I maintain
It's mine and mine it must remain.
He sold it to me at my altar
As I was reading in my psalter.
And by the true apostle Peter,
It won't be hers or your skin either
Without a judgment by the courts."
       My lords, Eustache d'Amiens exhorts
And urges and beseeches you,
570   Who understand what's just and true
To give the judgment. Which of these
By law and right should have the fleece,
The pastor or the pastoress
Or the saucy little servant lass?

II   *The Tresses*

This is the tale of the lady who, caught red-handed, succeeds in refuting the evidence and convincing her husband he has been dreaming. There are many tales of seeing-but-not-believing, and many variations of this particular tale. Granting that any time an oral tale travels from one country to another it loses some elements and acquires others, Bédier shows that the few links that the fabliau *Des Tresses* has with the Oriental tales are too fragile to establish a filiation. Indeed, the cut tresses are a primitive Germanic trait: according to Tacitus, adulterous women were chased from the marital domicile with their heads shaved (B chapt. 6). There are three Germanic versions of the tale, and another version is Neifile's tale from the seventh day in Boccaccio's *Decameron*. In French, there exist one other fabliau version, *De la Dame qui fist entendant son mari qu'il sonjoit* (MR 5:133, from MS. B) and an independent form of this tale by Jean de la Fontaine (B 195).

The fabliau itself might have been entitled "The Substitutions," for, at the climaxes of all three episodes, the lady provides a replacement for the object under contention: the mule for her lover, her friend for herself, and the mule's tail for her friend's hair. Like a magician, she substitutes everything to put her victim totally in her power, confusing him and rendering him incapable of distinguishing illusion from reality. Like a magician also, the author makes us react sympathetically to a lady who is cunning, manipulative, ruthless, and adulterous. Indeed, the whole blame is shifted to her husband, who deserves it, as the author explains in the last six lines of the fabliau. The author of our fabliau (MS D) was technically talented: in the original Old French, over half of the total rhymes are rich (matching at least one vowel and two consonant sounds), and a third match more than three sounds, often extending the rhyme to more than one syllable. (In French, unlike in English, homonyms are traditionally considered good rhymes.)

> Once there was a noble knight
> Whose courtly speech, chivalric might,
> And wisdom made him celebrated.
> In arms he was so dedicated
> To prowess that success forsook
> Him never in what he undertook.
> People he met on any quest
> Admired him and were impressed

So much that he gained such esteem,
10   People spoke of none but him.
While he was wise and valorous,
He also was magnanimous
When he had laid aside his shield:
A good man on or off the field.
His wife, who was of noble birth,
Loved more than anyone on earth
A knight who lived some five miles down
The highway, in another town.
Her lover visited rarely though,
20   Lest people see him come and go.
Whisperings of their affair
Had reached him, so he didn't dare
Confide with anyone in town.
He said it soiled a knight's renown
And that his love would be demeaned
To trust Richeut, the go-between.[1]
He didn't want to court disaster.
Besides, he had a clever sister
Who helped his cause by being chosen
30   In marriage to the lady's cousin.
The sister and the cousin dwelt
In that same town. The young man felt
Their house a proper place to meet,
Safe, convenient, and discreet,
Free from all scandal whatsoever,
To come and go and talk together.
      He summoned his lady there one day,
But when she came, she couldn't stay,
Because the lady hadn't been
40   There long before bad news came in:
Her husband would be coming home.
The lady knew the time had come
To leave. They said good-bye and kissed.
But first he had a small request,
Though what it was, he wouldn't tell,
And since she loved him very well,
She promised him that she'd comply.
And now he said he wished to lie
With her in bed, beside her lord.

---

[1] Richeut: famous prostitute in a fabliau by this name (B 304–09). Nykrog does not accept it as fabliau and calls it a novel (N 15).

50   "Nothing can keep me out," he swore.
        Courtly love had him in tow.
        He wouldn't let his love say no.
        She couldn't think of what to say
        And finally let him have his way.
        She hurried home and prepared the house
        For the arrival of her spouse,
        Pretending pleasure at his coming
        While all the while her heart was drumming
        From anger rather than from bliss.
60   I won't speak any more of this
        Except to say they drank and ate
        And went to sleep before too late.
        But one fact shouldn't be neglected:
        There was a stable which connected
        To where the couple went to sleep.
        Her lord had had it built to keep
        The horse he rode the oftenest
        And loved the most, for he assessed
        Its value right at forty pounds.
70   His other beasts and hawks and hounds,
        Except one mule, he could have spared,
        Lost, sick, or dead, and never cared.
        Now when the chimes struck nine o'clock
        And all the people there were locked
        In sleep, for people need their rest,
        The lover came upon his quest
        To find the lady where she slept.
        Beneath the windowsill he crept
        And clambered in, but had no way
80   Of knowing where the lady lay.
        He paused and listened; then he latched
        Onto the elbow which attached
        To the husband, who was not asleep.
        The lover had no time to leap.
        The husband seized him by the fist.
        Far off, in another house than this,
        The husband's men were sleeping soundly.
        However long, however loudly
        He called, they wouldn't come that night.
90   He threw himself with all his might
        Upon the man whose fist he caught.
        The lover held his own and fought
        With hand and foot as best he could.
        One of them pushed. The other pulled

Till both of them were tired out.
What a fool he'd been, the lover thought,
To get himself in such a fix.
They rested from their knocks and kicks
Inside the stable, where there stood
100   Up end a tub made out of wood.
The husband tilted it and stuck
Under it the man he took
To be an ordinary thief.
The lady ached from fear and grief,
Not for her lord's—for her lover's sake,
Seeing her husband hold and shake
The tub and beat the man like flax.
"Go for a candle! Get an ax,
And make it quick," he told his wife.
110   But she replied, "Not on your life.
Why God forbid I go back there
As dark as it is! I wouldn't dare.
I'd never find the kitchen door.
Give him to me, Lord. I'll make sure
This thief stays put. You'll never see
This rascal get away from me.
He can't get out of here. He's mine."
—"When he gets out, he won't go dine,"
The husband said, "not in this life."
120   —"Yes, sir, that's right," replied his wife,
"Don't pity him, don't save, don't spare—."
She grasped her lover by the hair
And seemed to hold it hard and tight.
Like it or like it not, the knight
Had to go groping through the house.
The lady let her lover loose
Before her lord got through the hall.
She brought the mule in from the stall
And grabbed it fiercely by the ears,
130   And just to make the scene appear
More credible, she shoved its head
Under the tub. Her husband sped
With fire and sword through the kitchen door.
"I'll have my captive's head!" he swore.
"His neck won't hold when I have struck it!"
But when he saw the mule and bucket
And wife holding on, he was dumbfounded.
"I swear to God," he cried, "Confound it,
I was a fool and a sucker, too.

140   Ever to take advice from you!
My fill of you is what I've had.
I'm worse than you, though. I was mad
To leave your lover when I had him.
You'd better follow him now, Madam.
It shouldn't give you cause for weeping,
But by St. Paul, you won't be sleeping
With me beside you anymore."
    At that he opened wide the door,
And out into the dark and cold
150   He thrust his wife. The lady strolled
To where her cousin and his spouse,
Her lover's sister, had their house
And met her love. By this time she
Had figured out a strategy
Whose cleverness was more than human.
She went to the house of a bourgeois woman,
A woman who could almost match her
In beauty, elegance, and stature,
And woke and rousted her from bed
160   And pleaded till the woman said
She'd help her in this time of need.
"Then go at once," she said, "God speed.
And do not stop until you've come
Into my house and to my room
To where my husband lies asleep.
Fall upon your knees and weep
As loud as you are able to.
No greater service you can do
Than this which you have promised me."
170   The woman went immediately
And knelt beside the husband's cover.
(The lady lay beside her lover,
Who spent the night doing all she wanted.)
The other woman loud lamented
Her wretched fate, Oh God, how wrong
She was! She never would prolong
Her life beyond this night, when trust,
Love, faith, and honor all were lost.
The lady's husband tossed and turned,
180   Groaned and ground his teeth and burned,
But though he tossed and counted sheep,
He couldn't toss himself to sleep.
Out of the bed the husband surged.
Never had he greater urge

To beat a woman than to beat
The one who knelt before his feet.
On each bare foot he strapped a spur,
And nothing else, confronting her
Naked but for the shirt he wore.
190 He came and seized her hair and bore
Her body down upon the ground.
About her head his fingers wound.
He yanked and jerked and pushed and pulled
Until his hands could hardly hold.
A hundred lines of blood he drew
Across her flanks and belly too,
Striking and raking with his spurs.
(The care she got from him was worse
Than what the lady was receiving
200 From her lover on that evening.)
He beat, and kept on beating her,
And the more he beat, the angrier
He got, and heaped her with abuse.
And when his anger was diffused,
He got back into bed again.
But little joy it gave him then:
Again the weeping had begun.
Much she repented what she'd done.
The woman wailed and sniffled and gulped,
210 For he had beaten her to a pulp.
Why should she laugh? This whole affair
Hadn't been much fun for her.
She cried out louder than her part
Required because she really hurt.
And neither was the knight amused
By her whose outcry so abused
His ears. He was enraged instead.
He jumped like a wild man from his bed,
Dripping sweat from grief and anger,
220 Then leaped before her with his dagger
And cut her tresses off. The shock
Was so severe for her it struck
Her dumb, and she could weep no more.
Her heart was weary to the core
And almost burst from so much weeping.
At last the husband left her, keeping
The tresses cut from off her head.
    The woman dragged herself, half dead,
To meet the lady, and reported

230 What happened, just as you have heard it.
   The lady promised her and swore
   She'd make her rich forevermore.
   As for her tresses, if she could get
   Them back, the woman needn't fret:
   She'd fix them to her head so well
   No man or woman could ever tell
   That they had suffered any violence.
   The lady left and walked in silence
   Unnoticed through the morning gloom
240 Until she came into her room,
   And there she saw her husband sleeping,
   Worn out and overworked from keeping
   Awake and angry, cutting hair.
   To waken him she did not dare,
   But sat in silence by the bed,
   Wondering where he could have hid
   The tresses stolen from her friend,
   Which, by the saints, would be avenged
   If she could get the best of him.
250 From end to end she searched the room,
   Looking for their hiding place,
   Then reached inside the pillowcase
   And groped and pulled the tresses out.
   Her sorrows you have heard about,
   But this was happiness she found.
   She left the room without a sound,
   Went through the stable door and cut
   The horse's tail off at the root,
   The horse on which her husband doted.
260 Now listen to an often quoted
   Appropriate proverbial sentence:
   "One sins; another does the penance";
   And so the horse endured the knife.
   The greatest pleasure of her life
   Was at that moment when she put
   The horse's tail which she had cut
   Into her husband's pillowcase.
   With everything arranged in place,
   Quietly, softly, lest he wake,
270 She slipped into the bed all naked
   And slept until the morning light.
   The bells at six awoke the knight,
   Who sat up in his bed and stared
   To see the lady lying there

Again beside him in his bed.
"Who brought you back?" the husband said,
"Who tucked you in with me?" —"But sir,
What place could there be properer
To lie in peace the whole night through
280   For your own wife than next to you?"
—"What!" he cried, "Don't you remember
Last night?—What happened in this chamber!
I caught your lover in the act
Right in this bed, to be exact.
By God, who hears the sinner's prayer,
What fit of folly, what despair
Brought you crawling back to me?
From this day on the door will be
Barred against you while I live.
290   I'm not the drunken lout you give
Me credit for, I thank the Lord."
—"As God's my help," the wife implored,
"You should speak better. I deny
And can refute that ever I
Served any other man than you
Or brought you shame. I swear that's true
By all the saints and sacraments.
You always used to make good sense,
But this is madness—every word!
300   Cross yourself! Call on the Lord!
Some evil spirit, ghost, or ghoul
Or devil has possessed your soul
And has misled you in the night."
—"You'd lead me by the nose all right
If I believed your words. Why, you
Would have me misbelieve what's true
And evident in my two hands.
Your skin should show how matters stand.
I certainly raked it with a will.
310   In fact I'm shocked to see you still
Alive. It's almost past believing."
—"God forbid I keep on living,"
Cried she who wept from make-believe,
"If for one hour I received
A beating from you—not a smack."
At that she threw her covers back
And showed her thighs and her white waist
And breasts and legs and flanks, and face
Without a dab of make-up on.

320 The husband looked her up and down,
But couldn't even find a bruise.
He was confounded and confused
And baffled. "Lady," he protested,
"I see a husband's time is wasted
Who beats and doesn't kill his wife.
I beat you to an inch of your life.
In honest faith I thought for sure
You wouldn't walk straight anymore.
If you were decent, if you were good,
330 Arise and walk you never could.
Devils healed you, didn't they?
You won't so easily find a way
To heal your shame: you've lost your tresses.
Two years—that's what my lowest guess is—
You'll wait before they grow back in."
—"My lord," she said, "this is a sin,
To slander me. I cannot eke
A grain of sense from what you speak.
If but one hair of my head was severed
340 For any anger whatsoever,
May God expel me from this place."
Her net of ribbons she unlaced
And let the tresses, which he thought
He'd shorn away, come tumbling out.
"Look here, my lord," the lady said,
"Last night I saw you get in bed
The wrong foot first and cross yourself
From right to left. I fear your health
Has gotten worse. It's no surprise
350 You're having trouble with your eyes.
Or else the vertigo or gout
Has put reality in doubt,
Or else it is the evil one,
Who clouds men's minds. When he has done,
And made great fools of clever men,
To nothing everything turns again.
When all the world is led astray,
His works will break and pass away—
For the love of God, sir, when you spoke,
360 Were you sincere? Is this a joke?"
The husband gasped and shook his head
And gaped and crossed himself for dread.
His wife, however, didn't swear
Or cross herself—she didn't dare!

But not the wealth of Aquitaine[1]
Could keep him quiet even then,
Because of the evidence he thought
He had: the tresses he had cut.
He reached inside the pillowcase
370   And almost fell upon his face
When out he pulled the horse's tail.
Now he saw all, in false detail.
"Oh God!" he cried, "What did I do
In one fell swoop last night I threw
Fifty pounds straight down the drain.[2]
I must have been berserk, insane
Or drunk to cut my horse's tail."
You should have seen the teardrops trail
In rivers down his cheeks and chin.
380   He was so shaken with chagrin,
He had no notion what to do.
He thought he was bewitched (That's true!
Bewitched is what he really was).
"Mary, most holy, pray for us,"
She wept; "I watch my lord go wander
Far from his wits and from his honor."
—"Lady," he said, "behold a wretch!
Don't hold me liable, I beseech,
For folly that you hear and see.
390   Lady, for God's sake, pity me!"
The lady answered, "Good my lord,
Before high God, I give my word,
I freely pardon your offenses.
God keep your body and your senses
From evil spirits and the devil.
Go to Vendôme, sir, so the evil
That clouds your mind may go away.
Do not forget. Do not delay.
Do not let business interfere.
400   Go to the Church of the Holy Tear,[3]
Gaze upon the Tear and pray,
And God will wash your scales away."
—"Lady," he said, "your word is true.

---

[1] Duchy in South of France.
[2] See line 69, where the horse is valued at only forty pounds. The Knight, in his despair, is exaggerating.
[3] Well-known pilgrimage for the blind in Vendôme, France.

Tomorrow morning that's what I'll do,
Because I dearly long to see!"
Nor did the lord forget. When he
Came back to her, he never breathed
A word, which, if she disagreed,
He didn't hasten to deny
410 And swear it was a dream, or lie.
      This story shows it isn't right
To put a wife outside at night
If she does folly with her flesh.
It only gives her means afresh
To load on shame and more distresses.
Thus ends my fabliau, *The Tresses*.

III   *The Priest Who Peeked*

GUERIN

This is another tale of seeing-but-not-believing. But here the husband actually watches as he is cuckolded. Like *The Tresses*, it has many analogues, most notably those which, according to Stith Thompson, share "The Enchanted Pear Tree" motif.[1] Larry Benson and Theodore Andersson, completing Stith Thompson's list, divided the analogues into two categories. In the first, the victim is persuaded by his wife that the optical illusion is caused by a magical tree. In the second, the husband is jealous and blind; when the lovers cavort in the pear tree, his vision is miraculously restored and his wife quickly convinces him that the restoration is due to her action with the lover. Boccaccio's version in *Decameron* (7.9) belongs to the first of these two types and Chaucer's *Merchant's Tale* to the second.[2]

Our fabliau resembles these tales on many points, but differs from them on others. The most obvious difference is the disappearance of the element of magic, possibly because of the down-to-earth nature of the majority of the French fabliaux, from which magic is excluded: the pastoral setting of the analogues is here replaced by the common dinner table.

The poem portrays the quick victory of cleverness in a quick style. For the deception to be effectively carried out, the peasant must not be allowed much time to think; nor must the audience, lest the trick seem too preposterous to matter. The action must move fast.

The tale ends with the status quo preserved and the marriage left intact. No tragedy has occurred, no particular sympathy has been aroused for one character or another; in spite of the reprehensible adulterous act, the audience can laugh without worrying about moral or social implications.

> If you will kindly listen well
> To my next tale, I'd like to tell
> A short and courtly fabliau
> As Guerin has it. Long ago

---

[1] *Motif-Index of Folk-Literature*, 2d ed., 6 vols. (Bloomington: Indiana University Press, 1955), motif 4:403.

[2] Larry Benson and Theodore Andersson, *Literary Context*, 203.

There lived a peasant who had wed
A maiden courteous, well-bred,
Wise, beautiful, of goodly birth.
He cherished her for all his worth
And did his best to keep her pleased.
10   The lady loved the parish priest,
Who was her only heart's desire.
The priest himself was so afire
With love for her that he decided
To tell his love and not to hide it.
So off he started, running hard.
As he came running through their yard,
The peasant and his wife were sitting
Together at the table eating.
     The priest neither called their name nor knocked.
20   He tried the door. The door was locked
And bolted tight. He looked around
And up and down until he found
A hole to spy through and was able
To see the peasant at the table,
Eating and drinking as she served.
The priest indignantly observed
The way the peasant led his life,
Taking no pleasure of his wife.
And when he'd had enough of spying,
30   He pounded at the doorway, crying,
"Hey there, good people! You inside!
What are you doing?" The man replied,
"Faith, sir, we're eating. Why not come
In here to join us and have some?"
—"Eating? What a lie! I'm looking
Straight through this hole at you. You're fucking."
—"Hush!" said the peasant, "Believe me,
We're eating, sir, as you can see."
—"If you are," said the priest, "I'll eat my hat.
40   You're fucking, sir. I can see that!
Don't try to talk me out of it.
Why not let me go in and sit?
You stand out here and do the spying,
And let me know if I've been lying
About the sight I'm looking at."
     The peasant leapt from where he sat,
Unlocked the door and hurried out.
The priest came in, turned about,
Shut the door and set the latch.

50   (This wasn't fun for the churl to watch.)
        Straight to the wife the parson sped,
        Spun her round and caught her head,
        Tripped her up and laid her down.
        Up to her chest he pulled her gown
        And did of all good deeds the one
        That women everywhere want done.
        He bumped and battered with such force
        The peasant's wife had no recourse
        But let him get what he was seeking.
60   And there the other man was, peeking
        At the little hole, through which he spied
        His lovely wife's exposed backside
        And the priest, riding on top of her.
        "May God Almighty help you, sir,"
        The peasant called, "is this a joke?"
        The parson turned his head and spoke:
        "No, I'm not joking. What's the matter?
        Don't you see: I have your platter.
        I'm eating supper at your table."
70   —"Lord, this is like a dream or fable.
        If I weren't hearing it from you,
        I never would believe it true
        That you aren't fucking my good wife."
        "I'm not, sir! Hush! As God's my life,
        That's what I thought I saw you do."
        The peasant said, "I guess that's true."
            That's how the peasant got confused,
        Bewitched, befuddled, and abused
        By the priest and by his own weak brain
80   And didn't even feel the pain.
        Because of the door, it still is said,
        "Many a fool by God is fed."

            Here ends the fabliau of the priest.
        The End: Amen.

IV *The Wife of Orleans*

This tale has several versions. In the Anglo-Norman *Du Chevalier et sa dame et un clerc* (MR 2:215), the protagonists are all noble, the clerk almost pines to death for love, and the lady betrays the husband she loves to save the clerk's life. Nykrog considers this so-called courtly version of our tale to be an inept attempt at blending a romance with a fabliau (N 66–68). La Fontaine was also inspired by this theme of "the husband cheated, beaten but happy" (B 298, 449–50). In addition to this "fabliau," Bédier cites a Provençal poem by Ramon Vidal and a German poem, all variations on the theme of the husband, cheated, beaten, and content, to show how a theme can be molded to fit the tastes of different classes of people.

The comic tale, in its austerity, has cut all connections with time and space in order to let the action fulfill itself in its humor. In view of that independence and our release from realities of space and time (and therefore of moral judgment), we can laugh without restraint and accept the final outcome of the story where everything is under control, and since the lover does not exactly ride off into the sunset at the end, we at least know that the marriage remains intact and that, if the husband is "cocu" (cuckold) and "battu" (beaten), he is also "content."

> A courtly romance I will tell
> Of a bourgeois' wife who used to dwell
> In the ancient town of Orléans.
> Her husband was from Amiens,
> A rich landowner who had made
> Money at usury and trade.
> He knew the ruses, tricks, and shifts
> For getting gold, and once his fists
> Closed on a thing, they held it tight.
> There came to town one summer's night
> A company of four young scholars
> With bookbags hanging from their collars.
> These boys were handsome, smart, and portly.
> They were big eaters too, and courtly.
> The people of the town all said
> They were fine fellows, nicely bred.
> The plumpest of the four was granted

10

To be a little bit romantic,
Not proud, but quiet as a mouse.
20 He frequented the husband's house.
The lady of the house delighted
In his acquaintance and invited
The boy to come and visit her
So often that the usurer
Determined that by some deception
He'd teach this scholar boy a lesson.
    For a long time he had the care
Of his young niece, who was living there.
He secretly called her aside
30 And promised her that if she spied
Upon the lady and her guest
He'd pay her with a pretty dress.
Meanwhile the scholar strove and pleaded
For friendship till the wife conceded:
She'd give him what he hungered for.
The niece was listening at the door.
She listened well enough to catch
The plot the wife and scholar hatched.
Back to her uncle the young girl ran
40 To tell him all about their plan.
The plan was, when the husband's work
Called him away, she'd call the clerk.
He'd come to the orchard gate and knock,
And she'd be waiting to unlock
And let him in when evening fell.
These tidings pleased the merchant well.
He called his wife and told her, "My
Affairs have summoned me and I
Must hurry immediately from here.
50 Take good care of the house my dear.
I don't know how long I'll be gone.
Be a good wife and carry on."
His wife replied, "I will, my Lord."
The husband gave his drivers word
That they would start the journey right
By leaving now. They'd spend the night
At a small inn three miles from there.
The wife did not suspect the snare.
At once she sent the clerk the news.
60 Meanwhile the rich man worked his ruse,
For when his drivers were in bed,
Back to the meeting place he sped.

That evening, as he lay in wait,
The lady stole to the orchard gate,
Opened it, and welcomed in
And held the man who should have been
Her lover, for she still believed
In what she hoped. She was deceived.
He who deceived her whispered low.
70   She hardly heard his quick, "Hello."
"I'm glad you're here," the lady said.
Along the orchard path she led
The way. He turned his face aside.
The lady peered around and spied
Beneath his hat where she detected
Something entirely unsuspected.
She hastily concluded that
Her husband hid beneath the hat
And set her mind to outmaneuver
80   This man who claimed to be her lover.
(Women have known how to deceive
Men ever since the time of Eve.
Not even Argus could guard women.)[1]
With whispered words she welcomed him in:
"It's good to have you by my side.
Be kind to me. I will provide
Some of my funds for you to pay
Your little debts if you will say
Nothing about this. Come, my love,
90   I'll hide you safely up above
In a small room I have the key to.
Be patient here and I will meet you
After my people have been fed.
When all of them have gone to bed,
I'll lead you to my bed downstairs.
Then nobody will know you're there."
—"Lady," he said, "that's very good."
Lord, how little he understood
Of what his lady thought about.
100 (A driver, though he plans his route,
Won't get there if the mule won't move.)
The husband's lot will not improve,
For when the merchant's wife had stuck

---

[1] Argus: the hundred-eyed giant whom Juno, wife of the god Jupiter, set to guard Jupiter's concubine, Io. With the help of the god Mercury, Io escaped.

Him in the attic, she turned the lock
And ran from the house to the orchard gate.
The clerk was there, though she was late.
She hugged and kissed and let him pet her.
This second comer had it better
Than he who reached the orchard first.
110   She let the one who had it worse
Stay in the upstairs room and stew
And brought the other safely through
The orchard to the hall which led
To the guest-bedroom door. The spread
Was folded back. They both got in.
She urged her scholar to begin
The game of love. He played so well
He wouldn't have given a hazel shell
For any other game, and neither
120   Would she, for they played well together.
They had good fun while the time sped.
They cuddled and kissed. At last she said,
"My friend, I have to go. Please stay
A little while. Don't go away.
Now I must go and be the lady
And see that the evening meal is ready.
We'll have our own meal by and by
Later tonight, just you and I."
The scholar nodded in assent.
130   She left him quietly and went
To the eating hall and did her best
To treat her husband's crowd like guests.
The lady put on quite a spread.
The people guzzled wine and fed
Themselves until they almost burst.
They finished and had not dispersed
When the lady asked for them to pay
Attention to what she had to say.
Her lord's two nephews were at the table,
140   A handyman who kept the stable,
A water boy, a cook, two grooms,
And three young girls who cleaned the rooms,
Not to mention the lady's niece.
"Ladies and gentlemen, God give you peace,"
The lady said, "Listen to me;
Lately you may have chanced to see
Hanging around this house a clerk
Who will not let me do my work.

He's begged for love in prose and rhymes.
150   I told him no a hundred times
Then learned I'd get no rest unless
My tactics changed, so I said yes.
I'd give him what he was begging for
As soon as my lord was out the door.
My husband's gone. God be his guide.
And now this clerk, this thorn in my side,
Has kept his part of the deal all right.
He thinks he's come to spend the night.
He's in the attic, waiting for me.
160   To each of you I guarantee
The finest wines in my husband's cellar
If you will fix this saucy fellow.
Arise, my people! Up to the attic!
Give him an answer that's emphatic.
Beat him up and beat him down,
Black and blue from toe to crown.
This is the last time in his life
He'll woo a self-respecting wife."
     As soon as the people there had heard,
170   Up they jumped with one accord.
One took a log, another a stick,
A third a pestle big and thick.
She gave the key. They rushed the stair.
"Don't let him get away from there!
Grab him before he's out the door."
(Some other teller could tell the score
Of all the blows that fell—I couldn't.)
"By God," they shouted, "Mr. Student,
We'll make you smart!" The elder brother
180   Wrestled him to the floor. The other
Laid hold of his uncle's overcoat
And yanked it over his face and throat
So that he couldn't utter a sound.
Then they really began to pound.
They were not bashful with the sticks.
He couldn't have gotten better licks
If he had paid ten sous apiece.
Both of the nephews and the niece
Sweated to give him many a blow
190   First above and then below.
It did no good to weep or shout.
Like a dead dog they dragged him out,
Dumped him on a pile of manure,

And clumped back through the kitchen door,
Then set themselves to drinking dry
The best of the husband's wine supply:
Red wines and white the lady poured.
Every laborer drank like a lord.
The lady took good wine and cakes
200   And a large candle of fine wax
And linen cloths with lace cutwork
And held good council with her clerk
All night until the night was spent.
True love decreed that when he went
She give him gifts of marks and sous.
She begged for other rendezvous
Whenever he could get there to her.
        At last the man in the manure
Moved his muscles to begin
210   The three-mile crawl back to the inn.
His drivers, when they saw him bruised
Showed much concern. They weren't amused,
But kindly asked him how he was.
"Bad," he said. "Now no more fuss.
Just take me home." He wasn't kidding.
They saddled up and did his bidding.
But after all, it did him good,
And put him out of his bad mood
To know his wife was free from stain.
220   He snapped his fingers at his pain.
If he survived the day, his wife
Would have his confidence all his life.
        He got home. When his wife perceived
His bruises, she was deeply grieved.
She poured an herb bath, put him in it
And eased his hurt in half a minute.
She asked him what on earth had happened.
"Lady," he said, "I have been destined
To pass through perilous straits alone
230   Whereby I've broken every bone."
His nephews told about the work
They had accomplished on the clerk
And how she led them to his lair.
"By gosh, she handled this affair
Discreetly and responsibly!"
Never more would the husband be
Suspicious, critical, or spying!
And never would she fail at lying

With him she loved until the day
240 He went to his own hometown to stay.

V   *Browny, the Priest's Cow*

JEAN BODEL

This seventy-two-line fabliau stands as a good example of compact narration. Most fabliaux whose humor rests on a verbal misunderstanding are short. The characters are neither named nor described: the peasant, his wife, and the priest are all that is needed for this tale. The setting is unspecified. Yet the author profits from this conciseness: the fabliau shows how a literal application can, as quickly as adding one plus one, bring about an unexpected result: two.

This fableor has been identified as Jean Bodel, the author of the *Jeu de St. Nicolas*, the *Chanson des Saisnes*, the *Congés*, and seven other fabliaux (including *Greed and Envy*, below). Nykrog (N 165) and Togeby (CH 11) cautiously propose that he may have been the inventor of the genre or at least one of its first composers. Nykrog wisely proposes that this attribution and identification can be reasonably presumed but not stated with scientific certainty. That a Jean Bodel wrote *Brunain* (*Browny*) is certain, but that this fabliau is our *Brunain* cannot be affirmed with full assurance in view of the multiplicity of fabliau versions, a caution that Johnston and Owen repeat (JO 94).

Helsinger chooses this fabliau to project his thesis that the humor in the fabliaux can originate from the allegory being turned inside out when the figurative becomes literal. Jean Bodel seems to be mocking allegory by making literal-mindedness successful: "In ... *Brunain* ... the letter does not kill; it instead nourishes" (CH 94).

Once, on blessed Mary's day,
A peasant took his wife to pray
And celebrate the mass in town.
Before the office, the priest came down
And turned to the people to deliver
His sermon: Blessed be the giver
Who gives for love of God in heaven.
God will return what has been given
Double to him whose heart is true.
10   "Dear wife!" the peasant said, "Did you
Hear what the parson up there said?
Whoever gives for God will get

The gift returned and multiplied?
What better use could we decide
For our cow, Berny, than to give her
To God through the priest? Besides, she never
Gives much milk." His wife said, "Good,
Since that's a fact, I think we should!"
They rose at once and left together.
20   When they got home, the farmer tethered
His cow and led her from the shed
And took her back to town and said
To the priest, whose name was Constant, "Sir,
Here's my cow Berny. I'm giving her
To you because I love the Lord."
He handed him the tether cord
And swore that she was all he had.
"That's wise indeed," the parson said,
Who night and day kept careful watch
30   For any handout he could catch.
"Well done, my son. In peace depart.
If all my parish were as smart
And sensible as you, there'd be
Plenty of animals for me."
        The farmer left and made his journey
Home to his wife. The priest gave Berny
To one of his clerks to be secured
To his cow, Browny, till they were sure
She felt at home. The clerk pulled hard
40   And brought the cow to the backyard
And got the priest's fat cow and tied
Berny and Browny side by side,
Then turned around and left the cows.
The parson's cow preferred to browse,
And bent her head to keep on chewing,
But Berny balked: no, nothing doing.
She pulled the tether good and hard,
Dragging her out of the priest's yard,
Past houses and hemp fields, over bridges,
50   Through meadows and hedges, hills and ditches
Till home she came to her own backyard.
The parson's cow, who held back hard
The whole long way, came dragging after.
The farmer looked outside, and laughter
Filled his heart. He gave a cheer.
"Hey!" he shouted, "Look, my dear!
See how the good Lord multiplies.

Here's Berny back and Berny twice—
Only the second's brown, and bigger!
60   That's two for one the way I figure....
And now our barn's not big enough."
    My lords, this fabliau is proof
It's foolish not to give all you own.
The good things come from God alone.
They are not buried in the ground.
Nothing ventured, nothing found,
And nothing multiplied. That's how
God blessed the man who risked his cow:
Two for the peasant, none for the priest,
70   And those who have the most, get least.

VI   *Greed and Envy*

JEAN BODEL

As Bédier notes (B 457), the story of this short fabliau was one of the favorite *exempla* of medieval preachers. Jean Bodel, its author, generally presents likable characters such as the peasant in *Browny, the Priest's Cow*. But this tale seems pessimistic and even threatening. However, as Nykrog judiciously points out (N 166), Bodel, by allegorizing this tale, avoids having to state that human beings are perverse and evil. Here, he is attacking vice not men.

In comparing this tale with *Browny . . .*, Cooke remarks, "The chance return of Blerain [Berny] stupefies because it did not have to happen; the evil outcome of the greedy and envious characters stuns like an unavoidable accident" (OF 124).

> After so many fabliaux,
> I'll tell you something true, because
> A raconteur whose repertoire
> Is fables only should be barred
> From court, my lords. Jongleurs should tell
> The gospel truth (sometimes), as well
> As lies. A skillful fableor
> For every two lines does one more
> That's better than the other two.
> 10   That's the truth, and this is, too:
>   There were two friends back long ago,
> About a hundred years or so,
> Who lived as bitter lives as can be.
> One was so consumed by envy
> He grieved if anyone received
> More than he did. The other's greed
> Was such that *more* would not suffice.
> Greed is worse than any vice.
> This is the way greed always rules:
> 20   It transforms people into fools.
> It lends at interest; then it waits
> To cut new deals at higher rates
> So greed can grow and greed can breed.

Envy's even worse than greed,
Roaming the world, anxious and frenzied.
    He who was greedy and he who envied
Were riding one day through a field
When all of a sudden there appeared
Martin, the patron saint of Tours.
30 He wasn't with them long before
He tried them out and got to test
The bad qualities they possessed
Planted firmly in their hearts.
At the point of land where the main road parts
To form two roads, there stood a chapel.
There the saint addressed the couple,
Whose lives were miserable as hell:
"My friends, it's time to say farewell.
I turn off here, but you can be
40 Happy you've kept me company.
My name's Saint Martin, by our Savior.
Go ahead: ask me a favor.
Whoever asks first gets his wish.
Whoever doesn't, I will dish
Our double to him what the first one got."
    The Greedy one decided not
To make a wish, since if he let
The other man wish first, he'd get
Two times the profit as the other.
50 "Go ahead, you ask, dear brother,"
He urged; "you lucky guy! You're sure
To get whatever you ask him for.
Go on! Wish for all you can!
Make yourself a wealthy man
For all your life. Wish! Wish your fill!"
The man who envied stayed stock still
And didn't wish for his desire
Because he'd rather die by fire
Than someone else get twice his sum.
60   Greed and Envy stood there dumb
A long, long time, until at last:
"What are you waiting for, God blast
Your hide?" the Greedy person swore;
"I'm bound to come out two times more
Rich than you, so you wish first.
Wish! Or I'm going to beat you worse
Than they beat the donkey off the bridge!"
—"All right, all right, all right, I'll wish!"

The man who always envied said,
70   "Before you beat me in the head.
You think I'll wish for cash. You count
On getting double my amount—
Well, not if I can have my way
You won't! Saint Martin, sir, I pray
That I may lose one of my eyes.
And him lose two. So he'll get twice
My wish, but not in cash—in pain!"
      Losing his eyes was all Greed's gain.
That's how their wishes came to be.
80   Out of four eyes, they lost three.
The wish was made, the Saint complied,
Made one man blind, and one, one-eyed.
But don't blame me. They got no more
Nor less than they were asking for.

VII The Villager and His Two Asses

The word *vilain* (here translated *villager*) has no precise equivalent in modern English. It means *commoner* but is much more frequently used and lacks the good connotations implied by such phrases as *House of Commons* and *the common man*. *Farmer* or *peasant* often translates it well (*Browny*), but not in this case, where the *vilain* is an urban, rather than a rural, commoner. Sometimes, as in *Aloul* (ll. 402–403) and *Knights, Clerks, and the Two Churls*, the word is so derogatory that only *churl* will do, or even *lout* (*The Fisherman from Pont-sur-Seine*, l. 158). The variety of possible translations of *vilain* reflects the various attitudes towards commoners in the fabliaux. If the *vilain* is shrewd, he will be drawn sympathetically, but he may also be repugnant because of his ugliness, brutality, or stupidity (N 129). Some commoners are jovial and intelligent, such as our farmer in *Browny*. Others are repulsive because of the filth in which they are living (*De la Crote*, MR 3:46; *De la Coille noire* MR 6:90). The unforgivable sin for a *vilain* is to try to elevate himself, undeservedly, out of his social class: *Berangier* (see below) stands as a good example of the merciless response to such social pretensions. Strongly opposed to interclass marriage, the fabliaux uphold the status quo.

Class pretension implies a certain amount of pride, a vice which, if unfounded, is condemned severely in the fabliaux: misplaced pride motivates Guerin's animosity against the peasant's son in *Berangier*, and such a pride is also the vice under attack in this fabliau (l. 50).

> Once there lived in Montpellier
> A villager who every day
> Gathered dung which he wrapped in packs
> And bore on two fine asses' backs.
> One day, as soon as he had loaded
> His asses with manure, he goaded
> Them into town and drove them through
> The narrow streets with much to do.
> He shouted, "Git up! Move along,"
> So loudly that before too long
> They reached the spice retailers' quarter.
> Apprentices were beating mortars,
> And when he smelled the fragrant spice,
> A world of gold could not entice

10

The man to take one step ahead.
He fell, and lay there looking dead.
The people there then felt a great
Uneasiness at the man's fate
And murmured, "For the love of Pete,
20   Look at that dead man in our street."
Not one could tell another why.
The asses meanwhile were standing by
In the middle of the road, for such
Is an ass's nature. It won't budge
Unless it feels its master's goad.
    A man who was standing up the road
Had seen the driver have his stroke.
He sauntered down the street and spoke
To those who stood around the man.
30   "Sirs," he said, "if no one can
Or wants to cure this man, I will
For what he gives me when he's well."
To this a citizen replied,
"Cure this man, and I'll provide
Twenty sous from my own pocket!"
—"Thanks," said the other man, "I'll take it."
At that he took the driver's fork,
Which was used to drive the beasts to work,
And forked some dung the size of a rose
40   And brought it to the stunned man's nose.
As soon as the flavor of manure
Had made the spice smell disappear,
He blinked his eyes and up he sprang.
"I'm fit as a fiddle now," he sang.
Happy now and overjoyed,
He made a vow that he'd avoid
Forever the avenue of spices.
    The moral's clear, and my advice is:
Though you be humble as manure,
50   Stick to your nature. Pride is sure
To make you sick; Nature will cure.

VIII   *Knights, Clerks, and the Two Churls*

This short tale is a rather complicated one. While there are many likable and intelligent peasants in the fabliaux (*The Fisherman, The Partridges, Browny*) these two *vilains* are quite despicable. The author's intentions, however, are not very transparent. His use of the word *vilain* instead of *paysan* seems quite deliberate, for he is quite precise in his definition (ll. 43, 44): "low-life" is to be judged on attitudes, manners, and sensitivity. Those, like our peasant in the *Villager and His Two Asses,* who are insensitive to beauty should stay where they are and not foul up beautiful spots.

We should note that the description of the *locus amoenus,* or pleasant place which inspires merriment, good cheer, and love, is a common motif in courtly literature. Those too insensitive to appreciate such thoughts are here invited to stay out, no matter what their social standing: "peasant, knight or earl."

> Two knights were riding, side by side.
> One rode a pinto, the other a pied.
> They came upon a grassy glade,
> Covered with flowers, cooled by the shade
> Of willows, watered by a brook.
> There they paused to take a look:
> "Dear God, this place would be ideal
> To spread a picnic. What a meal!
> With nothing but a jug of wine,
> Patés and pastries, a man could dine
> Better than in a banquet hall
> At table staring at a wall."
> Having said that, the knights rode on.
>   Two merry students came along,
> And when they reached the lovely glade,
> They spoke the way clerks speak. One said,
> "Whoever had a woman here,
> One that he loved, tender, dear,
> Could have some very pleasant fun."
> —"He'd be a fool," said the other one,

10

20

"A feeble-hearted, cowardly cur,
Not to have his way with her."
When they had spoken, on they passed.
    Two churls came tramping through the grass,
On their way home from market sales,
Carrying with them picks and flails,
And took their ease beneath an oak.
The way churls speak is how they spoke:
One said, "Sir Foosher, here we sit.[1]
30   What a perfect place to shit!
My friend, let's take a shit right here."
—"Yeah!" said the other, "Good idea!"
Then each churl strove and strained and did it.
    This tale is sign and proof and credit
That there's no pleasure in the world
Other than shitting for a churl.
Since churls go fouling with their feces
All the fair and lovely places
Merely for the fun of it,
40   I swear by God and Holy Writ,
John the Baptist, James and Moses,
I wish they'd shit it out their noses.
Churl isn't necessarily *peasant*.
No one's a churl if his soul isn't.
It's churlish deeds that make the churl,
Whether he's peasant, knight or earl.
From churlishness may God protect us,
Ransom, save and resurrect us.

---

[1] Sir Foosher: the Old French name (spelled *Fouchier*) divides into *Fou*, probably meant to be onomatopoetic, and *chier, to shit.*

IX   *The Partridges*

This amusing short tale exemplifies the narrative economy and simplicity of the fabliau. Keeping his tale brief and straightforward, our anonymous author hints at more than he tells, never stating that the wife and priest are lovers, but letting us infer their intimacy from their first encounter (lines 78–83) and infer the wife's cleverness in transforming the priest's guilty conscience into terror.

The thirty-eight line description of the wife's succumbing to the temptation of gluttony is a masterpiece of the genre, resembling, as Nykrog points out, A. Daudet's Reverend Father Gaucher (N 157).

The tale is also very rich despite its simplicity. As Howard Helsinger demonstrates, the wife and the priest are readily interpreted allegorically as Gluttony and Lust (CH 95, 96).

> I'm used to telling fabliaux,
> Not fables, which is why I chose
> To tell what really did take place
> One day. A peasant caught a brace
> Of partridges behind his hedge.
> Eager to prepare his catch,
> He told his wife, who was well skilled
> In cooking partridges, to build
> The fire up. She got it lit,
> 10   Put on the birds and turned the spit.
> He ran to get the priest to come,
> But took so long returning home
> The birds were done before he came.
> His wife removed them from the flame,
> Pinched some skin and took two bites.
> (She dearly loved her appetites
> And never liked to skimp or save
> Gifts that the good Lord freely gave:
> Eating made the gift complete.)
> 20   Bravely she attacked the meat
> And ate two wings immediately,
> Then ran outside the house to see
> Whether her man was getting near;
> No one in sight, the road was clear,

So once again into the house
She ran and finished off the grouse.
So much for it. One grouse was gone.
She thought about the other one:
She really ought to eat it, too.
30   Besides, she knew what she would do
If anybody asked. She'd say
Cats came, grabbed both, and ran away
Before the birds were on the table—
That way she'd get out of trouble.
She ran outside again to peer
Way down the road—was her husband near?
And when she couldn't see him yet,
Her tongue began to twitch and fret
Over the bird she hadn't had.
40   Her appetite would drive her mad
Unless she had one little peck.
Carefully, she dislodged the neck,
Deliberately ate off the meat,
And licked her fingers clean and neat.
"Alas," she said, "what shall I do?
What shall I say if I eat this, too?
But how can I keep from eating still?
I want it, don't I? So I will!
I don't care. Let the worst befall.
50   I have to eat. I'll eat it all."
She meditated thus until
The meat was gone and she was full.
     And now the man delayed no more.
He came in, shouting at the door,
"Those partridges—how do they look?"
—"Alas, we've had some rotten luck:
Cats came," she said, "and ate them each."
He screamed and charged and tried to reach
His wife, assaulting her with cries
60   Of wrath and would have gouged her eyes,
But, "Wait!" she cried, "Joke. Joke! Enough!
Behind me, Satan. Scram. Get off!
I covered them to keep them hot!"
—"Fine thanks from me you would have got,"
He said, "by Lazarus the good!
Get down my cup of Spanish wood
And get my whitest coverlet.
I'll spread it on my cape and set
Them by the trellis on the dew."

70   —"Then take your knife out when you do
        And sharpen it upon that stone
        So it can slice through skin and bone,
        And don't stop grinding till it can."
        He stripped to the waist and out he ran,
        Waving the naked blade on high.
            After a while the priest came by,
        Planning to eat some partridges.
        He gave the wife a tender kiss
        And tenderly he said, "Hello."
80   The wife's response was simple: "Go!
        Get out, my lord!" she said. "Go. Flee!
        I wouldn't want to have to see
        Your flesh dismembered, maimed, or marred.
        My husband's out there in the yard
        Honing his knife. Do you know what
        He means to do? He means to cut
        Your balls off if he catches you.
        God help you, sir!" —"God help you, too,"
        The priest replied, "but what is this?
90   I came to eat some partridges
        For lunch, the two your husband snared."
        —"By all the saints," the wife declared,
        "No birds in here, believe me, sir.
        I'd like to feed you if there were.
        I'm sorry for the fix you're in,
        But look at my husband, sharpening,
        Honing and polishing his knife."
        —"I see," he answered. "By my life,
        There must be truth in what you say."
100   The priest did not prolong his stay.
        Hurriedly he left the house.
        And now the woman called her spouse:
        "Gumbut! Hurry! As fast as you can!"
        —"What's wrong with you?" —"God help you, man,
        You'll learn what's wrong and soon enough.
        If you can't run your britches off,
        You'll be the worse for it. The priest
        Took both your birds. There goes your feast."
            The man went wild. His knife was out.
110   He chased the chaplain with a shout:
        "Come back, you wretched priest! God knows
        You'll never get away with those.
        Come back!" he shouted and repeated.
        "You're leaving with them good and heated.

Give up! I'll catch you in the end!
Is that the behavior of a friend—
To keep them to yourself? It isn't!"
The priest looked back and saw the peasant
Gaining on him every second.
120   And when he saw the knife, he reckoned
That death, dishonor and disaster
Were chasing him. So he ran faster.
Gumbut ran, too—he must release
The captive partridges from the priest,
Who ran for his life and with a last
Leap cleared his door and shut it fast.
     The peasant turned and trudged home now
And reasoned with his wife: "Now how
On earth—will you tell me this?—
130   Did you lose those partridges?"
—"So help me God," she said, "the priest
Begged me, when he came to feast,
To satisfy a little whim,
And show him, for the love of him,
The partridges, and so I brought
Him to the partridges you caught,
Where they were covered, safe and hot;
But then the priest reached in the pot
And grabbed the partridges and fled.
140   I didn't follow him. Instead,
I let you know immediately."
—"Ah ha!" the peasant said. "I see.
Let's just forget it for a while."
That's how the parson was beguiled,
And Gumbut, who had caught the birds.
     The point of these poetic words
Is women live but to conceal
The truth. They turn what's false to real.
What's true, they transform to a lie.
150   Thus ends my fabliau. Goodbye.
I'm finished now. That's all there is
About the peasant's partridges.

X   *Hearmie*

The fabliau *Estula* ("Are you there?") is one of many whose plot relies on words rather than on actions. The *quiproquo*, the misunderstanding, is amplified to what Cooke calls a "narrative or extended pun" (OF 158). The misunderstandings here are verbal and physical since the priest, in the grotesque scene where he is carried piggyback to the miraculous spot where his holy services are needed, is mistaken for a sheep. As this point (ll. 96 onward), the scene is reminiscent of *The Partridges* where the priest believes he has been betrayed and flees in terror.

The moral of this fabliau is indeed very appropriate. The author of this endearing tale is careful to portray the two thieves very sympathetically: they are orphans (l. 2), they live in abject poverty (ll. 4, 11–14), and they use their intelligence and craftiness to survive (l. 15). The fact that they are pitted against a rich but stupid neighbor enhances our sympathy for them. So when, at the end, the author states that he believes in the cyclical nature of fortunes and in some kind of justice which will make joy follow sadness, we feel that the two likable thieves deserve their good fortune, for they have suffered too long from lack of joy and laughter (ll. 133–4).

> Once long ago there lived two brothers
> Without a father's aid or mother's,
> No one to help or recommend,
> And poverty their closest friend
> And only friend through thin and thick.
> She is the one who makes men sick
> To whom she ever clings and cleaves:
> There never was a worse disease.
> Thus these two brothers lived together
> 10   Sharing affliction with each other.
> One night when they endured the worst
> Of gnawing hunger, cold and thirst
> (These ills are never far away
> When one is poverty's protegé),
> They thought and turned their wits about
> Seeking a way to struggle out
> From under the authority
> Of their oppressor, poverty.

Near where these brothers lived there dwelt
20   A man notorious for his wealth,
But they were poor. This wealthy sot
Had cabbages growing on his lot
And flocks of sheep inside his pen.
They started. Poverty makes men
Become impetuous and bolder.
One threw a sack upon his shoulder,
The other took his knife in hand.
They climbed the fence as they had planned.
One brother reached the garden gate,
30   Went in and didn't hesitate
To cut a cabbage head or four.
The other reached the sheepfold door,
Opened it and sidled through.
His work was going nicely too.
He groped to find the fattest sheep.
Someone inside, not quite asleep,
Awoke because he thought he heard
A gate hinge creaking in the yard.
The master called: "Go to the door,
40   My son, and take a look. Make sure
There's nothing going on around
The yard or pen, and call the hound."
Hearmie was the hound dog's name,
But this night, luckily for them,
He'd gone out somewhere for a run
And wasn't home. The master's son
Called, "Hearmie! Hearmie!" out the door.
The man in the sheepfold answered, "Sure,
I *hear* you. I don't see you though."
50   The yard outside was black as a crow.
The master's son could not perceive
Who answered him, but he believed
It was the dog. He didn't stay
To hear what else the dog might say
But cautiously stepped back inside
And shut the front door, terrified.
The master called, "What's the matter now?"
—"Sir, by my mother's love, I vow,
Hearmie spoke to me out there."
60   —"What? Our dog?" —"He did, I swear!
If my word's not enough for you,
Call him yourself. You'll hear him, too."
The father fidgeted to know

If this phenomenon was so.
He rose, stepped out the door and cried,
"Hearmie!" Again the man outside,
Who couldn't see, said, "Yeah, I hear!"
The father shook with awe and fear.
"By God in heaven and his saints,
70 Of all the marvelous events
I ever heard, this beats them all.
Run to the rectory and call
The priest. Tell him this wondrous thing,
Make him come here and have him bring
Some holy water and a Bible."
The son, as fast as he was able,
Ran to the house beside the church.
He didn't dawdle on the porch
But burst in where the parson sat.
80 "Arise, Sir Parson, grab your hat!
Come hear what happened in our back yard,
The strangest thing you ever heard!
Put on your stole, bring holy water!"
The priest replied, "Now what's the matter
With you? Look at my feet: they're bare!
You know I can't go way out there."
The young man answered, "You can too!
Get on my back. I'll carry you."
Without another word, the son
90 Bent over, and the priest got on,
Carrying his stole. They raced
Back home. The young man in his haste
Cut down a hill along a road
One of the thieves had gone for food.
The thief with cabbage in his sack
Saw the white priest on the son's back
And thought it was the stolen sheep
His brother was bringing from the keep.
He called out, grinning with delight,
100 "Got something good there?" —"You're darn right!"
Replied the son, who wrongly thought
His father was asking *whom* he brought.
"Quick," said the thief, "you throw him down.
I've got my knife. It's honed and ground.
Last night at the forge I sharpened it.
It won't be long till his throat is slit!"
When he heard that, the parson thought
He was the victim of a plot

Against his life. He lost his head,
110   Dropped from the young man's back, and fled,
But as he fled, his surplice snared
Upon a stick, and it stayed there.
He didn't stop, he didn't pause.
He left it hanging where it was.
    The man with the cabbage he had taken
Was almost as severely shaken
As he whom he had scared away.
What had happened he couldn't say,
But since the white thing on the stake
120   Was hanging there, he thought he'd take
A look. A surplice!—his to keep!
The other brother hauled the sheep
Upon his back from the corral
And got together with his pal
Who had the cabbage in his sack.
Both had a load to carry back.
They figured it was best to cut
Their visit short. Home in their hut,
Close by the wealthy man's abode,
130   The brother with the cabbage showed
His winnings off. They carried on,
Joking and laughing till the dawn,
For laughter, which too long had been
Absent from there, was theirs again.
    God works while others do the sleeping.
Those who rise laughing lie down weeping.
Those who sorrow in the evening
Rise happy and forget their grieving.

XI   *The Fisherman from Pont-sur-Seine*

This fabliaux stands as a good example of a tale whose well-proportioned plot moves steadily towards its conclusion. It presents to us a jovial peasant who attracts our sympathy because of his intelligence and wit and a wife who is satirized because of her lust and hypocritical modesty (ll. 52–62). Antifeminist satire, especially focusing on women's sexual appetites, is not uncommon in the fabliaux, although Muscatine (M), believes that it might be regarded less a satire than a celebration of the phallus, a literary veneration of sexual hedonism. It is a tale about male domination and the fear that castration would reverse the roles in the family.

The tale also stands as an excellent example of Roy J. Pearcy's thesis that the language used by tricksters is frank and obscene whereas the one used by dupes is essentially euphemistic (contrast lines 43–51 spoken by the husband with the wife's reply in lines 54 and 58!). In our fabliau *The Maiden Who Couldn't Hear . . .*, figurative language also masks a strong hypocrisy about sexual matters. According to Pearcy, "Dupes employ euphemisms to render less immediate a reality their hypocrisy will not allow them to admit" (CH 181). Once that reality is made evident, the dupe can either admit that evidence in frank language, as the wife does here (l. 195), or be so blind that the process of revelation passes him completely by, as in *The Lady Leech*, where figurative expressions, although brutally direct for those who understand them, remain obscure to the husband.

> Last week I heard of a fisherman
> Who lived in the town of Pont-sur-Seine.
> The man got married in a heat.
> The marriage brought him wine and wheat
> And twenty sheep and five fat cows.
> The little darling and her spouse
> Loved each other very dearly.
> Every morning, bright and early,
> He took his boat upon the Seine
> And brought good money home again.
> Every night, when he had fished,
> He sold and ate up all he wished

10

And fed her fish and meat and gravy.
He was the lord, and she the lady
Of him and all his worldly goods.
He lived the way a gentleman should
And laid his lady very well.
(Whoever doesn't will compel
A young wife's love to travel on.
20   Joy, too, will leave, when love is gone.
A young and well-fed, healthy wife
Wants frequent fucking all her life.)
     One day they lay in bed. His prick,
Which was well formed and long and thick,
Was sticking out, and as they kissed,
She held it wrapped inside her fist.
It wasn't saggy at her touch.
"My lord, I love you twice as much,"
She said, "as Peter Boy, my brother,
30   Or as my father or my mother,
Or little sister, Elenore."
—"I wouldn't believe you if you swore,"
He answered. "You don't even love
Me half what you'd have me believe.
Saying you love me is a trick."
—"I'm not!" she answered, "by Saint Nick.
You love me, dear. That's why I love you.
You give me food and clothes enough. You
Feed me when I'm hungry, too.
40   And yesterday you bought a new
Blue coat for me and a blue dress."
—"You'd love me, dear, a whole lot less
If that were all that I could do:
Love would leave, and so would you
Unless I screwed you well. You'd spurn
Me worse than you would a dog. I earn
Your love by working for your pleasure.
Never for finery or treasure
Do women love their lords the way
50   They do for screwing's what I say."
     The woman puckered. Then she pouted.
"Fie! Me? No, God forbid," she shouted;
"I'd never love because of that.
Your business bothers me. In fact,
If I could dare to keep you out,
I wouldn't let you butt about
With your repulsive outhouse stick.

Me like it? No! It makes me sick.
There's nothing viler. Vile! I hate it.
60   I wish to God that a pig ate it—
Except you'd bleed to death, I mean."
—"Sweet heart, you'd be in trouble then,
For if I lost my prick," he said,
"Bad luck, I might as well be dead;
You'd never love me anymore."
—"Yes, I would! More than before!"
Said she who was lying through her teeth:
"I hate to feel, ugh, underneath
Your clothes that filthy hang-and-swish
70   Swinging between your legs. I wish
That God in Heaven would see fit
To let a mongrel choke on it."
        By now the man could not decide
Whether she told the truth or lied,
Till a strange incident occurred
That gave him means to test her word.
        Early one morning he left his wife
And took his net and fishing knife,
Put his hand upon the oar,
80   Pushed the boat off from the shore,
And went out fishing on the Seine
To where the wide main channel ran
Strong and swift. There he found
The body of a priest who'd drowned,
Floating gently down the Seine,
Atoning for a certain sin:
A knight had suspected him of treason
And hated him for this one reason:
His wife. Jealousy had struck!
90   It made him watch and spy and look
Until he found their flesh atwin,
Male above the female skin,
Naked to naked. He caught them there.
The priest leapt out, prick in the air,
Into the Seine. He tumbled down.
The Seine was deep. He had to drown.
He didn't stop right there, however.
The fisher found his corpse down river,
And when it reached him, naked and dead,
100   He thought of his wife, what she had said—
That nothing in the world existing
Was so repugnant or disgusting

As was his penis to his wife.
At that he took his fishing knife,
Clipped the priest's penis at the root,
Washed and dried it in the boat,
Put it in his lap, and fished
Till he had all the fish he wished,
And then returned to his own place,
110   Pulling a long and woeful face
As if he meant to end his life.
Out to greet him came his wife.
"Sister," he shouted to her, "back!
All joy is gone. Alas, alack!
I'm dead, defeated, ruined, done.
Three knights assailed me. All I won
From them was this: they let me choose
Which member I preferred to lose:
If they deprived my eyes of sight,
120   I would have lost all joy and light.
If they had taken off my ears,
Men would have talked of it for years.
And so I told them, go ahead
And take my prick—because you said
It was the thing you most abhorred."
He tossed the penis on the floor.
She looked it carefully up and down
And saw that it was big and round
And recognized it for a prick.
130   "Fie!" she said. "You make me sick.
God shorten all your days on earth.
I hate you. Now your body's worth
Nothing. Nothing. Nothing's worse.
I'll go my way. You go yours."
—"What? Dear sister, didn't you say
That you would never, in any way,
Hate me if my prick were gone?
Now I'm confused. What's going on?"
—"I'll say what I've said repeatedly:
140   Your thing doesn't mean a thing to me.
Your loutishness is what I abhor.
I won't sleep with you anymore."
She called to her serving girl, her niece,
Who used to live in town: "Bernice!
Go out and round up every cow.
Bring them through the gate, and now!
Out in the back is where I'm going."

Out in the fields the beans were growing,
Ready to be harvested.
150 Listen to what the woman did:
"Bernice, Bernice," he heard her shout,
"Come on and hold your apron out.
Gather the best beans in the harvest;
I'll make sure I get the largest.
I'll fill my blouse till they burst out.
I won't leave any for the lout
As long as I can stuff them in it."
    Her husband shouted, "Wait a minute!
When we wed in holy church,
160 I swore, for better or for worse,
Dear love, to love you faithfully.
Here's twenty-six sous, still with me:
Come take your half. It would have been
A treacherous and grievous sin
For me to cheat you of your share.
Come split the total, fair and square.
Take half and leave the rest to me."
    At this, the wife came back to see.
She put her hand beneath his belt
170 And groped inside his pants and felt
A robust prick, which palpitated.
She pressed it with her palm and weighed it
And felt its hardness and its heat.
For joy her heart skipped half a beat:
"What's this I feel inside your britches?"
—"My prick, which stretches up and reaches,
Just the way it used to do."
—"What? Are you joking?" —"No, it's true!"
—"But how did you recover it?"
180 —"God in his mercy has seen fit
To make me whole again and save me.
He never wanted you to leave me."
    She hugged him now and kissed and licked,
And all the time she held his prick.
"Ah, my brother! My dear, sweet friend,
Today you frightened me no end.
I never had such a fright before."
She hugged and kissed and kissed some more,
Then called her servant from the house.
190 "Bernice," she called, "bring back the cows!"
Again she cried out, loud and clear,
"Bring back the cows! Come, bring them here!

My husband's prick has been restored.
The Lord has done it! Praise the Lord!"
    My lords, he who believes his mate,
Unless his eyes corroborate
Is a fool. In short, this tale expresses
How any bride whom fortune blesses
With a great lord, no matter how
200   Handsome, praised and well endowed
With wit and though a knight more noble
Than Sir Gawain and the Round Table,
If he should be emasculated,
Will not be happy till she's traded
Him for the worst slave in the yard,
Provided she can be assured
Of regular and frequent laying.
But if the ladies say I'm lying,
I'll have to let them have their say.
210   My story's finished anyway.

XII   *The Lady Leech*

In *William of the Falcon*, the lady discovers the power of the word, how its interpretation can fluctuate between the concrete and the symbolic almost at will, how its lack of absolute meaning can correspond to a lack of individual personality, and even how, unconnected to morality and to reality, it can justify a reprehensible act. In *The Lady Leech* the lady discovers the power of the sustained metaphor which brings about justice and symmetry in the deserved punishment of the husband who bragged loudly that no woman could ever deceive him (ll. 1–4).

The lady could have been satisfied with merely cuckolding her husband, since all she had to do was to prove her husband wrong (ll. 5–8). But by describing her adultery to her husband's face, in long metaphorical detail, as a leaching, or medical bleeding, she gets double revenge.

The two highpoints of the fabliau — the cuckolding of the husband and the allegorizing of the event by the lady — are identically marked by a crescendo rhythm, mounting to a frenetic pace. When things calm down, the author blames the husband's foolishness in claiming superiority over women (ll. 101–4); she tested him, and won (l. 98), but she also felt the need to tell him metaphorically of her victory (l. 100). We agree with him and with Pearcy, who praises that verbal composition as "an extensive allegory rivaling that at the conclusion of *Le Roman de la Rose*" (CH 179).

> The life of a businessman I'll tell
> Who one day boasted like a fool
> No woman could deceive him, but
> Too bad for him—his wife found out.
> The more she pondered it, the more
> She was annoyed. At last she swore
> However much the man might spy,
> She'd prove his foolish boast a lie.
> One day the boaster and his spouse
> Were sitting quietly in their house
> Upon a bench. A rogue came knocking,
> A noble rogue and quite good looking,
> Except that he resembled more
> A woman than a man. He wore
> A linen dress, loosely fit,

10

And saffron wimple. He brought a kit
Of tubes and bleeding cups, and sailed
Inside as bold as brass and hailed
The businessman and said, "Hello, sir.
20   May heaven's grace be ever closer
To you and everybody here."
—"God bless you, too, my lovely dear,"
The husband said, "Come sit by me."
—"No thank you, sir!" he said, "You see,
I don't feel tired, not at all.
Here I am, madam, at your call.
You summoned me here, didn't you?
What are you wanting me to do?"
The wife was not abashed by this.
30   "That's right," she said, "my dear young miss.
Please come upstairs for a few instants.
I need professional assistance."
She told the businessman, "Don't worry.
We'll be right down again. We'll hurry.
I've got the gout. My kidneys, sir,
Get goutier and goutier.
When I've been bled, they'll feel much better."
Lady and rogue went up together.
She shut the door and turned the lock.
40   The rogue grabbed hold of her and rocked
Her body backwards, stretched her flat,
And screwed her three times. After that,
When they'd had all the fun they wished,
Screwed, embraced, and hugged and kissed,
They rose and went downstairs again.
The rascal was no fool, for when
They got downstairs, he turned to say
A word to the husband: "Sir, good day."
—"My dear," he answered, "God protect you.
50   And you, my lady, I'll expect you
To pay this girl a goodly sum
Since she's been good enough to come
And give you freely of her service."
—"What's that to you, sir? Don't perturb us
With money talk," the lady said.
"You talk as though you've lost your head.
We two can settle this affair."
The rascal left them then and there
And took his bleeding instruments.
60   The lady sat upon the bench.

Red in the face and out of breath.
"Madam, you look worn to death.
That treatment must have been too long."
—"Thanks, sir. Whew! You aren't far wrong.
    I strained as hard as a woman could.
A hundred strokes. It did no good.
I couldn't bleed. She thumped me till
My flesh was soft as dough, and still
I didn't bleed a single drop.
70   Three times she took me, and atop
My loins she placed two heavy tools
And struck me blows so long and cruel
I felt the pangs of martyrdom,
But not a drop of blood would come.
Such hard and frequent blows she struck,
I would have died had not good luck
Brought comfort with a soothing salve.
Whoever had this salve would have
Relief and every anguish eased.
80   When all the hammering had ceased,
This easeful ointment she applied
Upon my wounds both deep and wide
Until it cured me of my ache.
This medicine was good to take.
Such doctoring could be endured!
And yet, don't get me wrong, my lord:
This ointment issued from a dropper
Down through a pinhole in a stopper
That was grotesque and dark and rude.
90   But glory be, the salve felt good!"
—"My dear," the businessman replied,
"I fear you must have almost died.
That must have been effective ointment."
    She told her medical appointment
As one long joke he didn't get.
She gloried in her sinning, yet
No shame she suffered from her jest.
Though she had put him to the test,
She did not feel the game was won
100   Until she told him what she'd done.
That's why I say that any man's
A fool who swears by head and hands,
"No woman makes a fool of me.
I keep close watch. It couldn't be."
This country doesn't have, however,

A man so wise, a man so clever,
Despite his prying, spying, snooping,
Who can avoid a woman's duping,
Since such a husband did not doubt
110   The woman with the kidney gout.

XIII *The Maiden Who Couldn't Hear Fuck Without Having Heartburn*

Several fabliaux deal with the theme of seduction, with characters identifying body parts by euphemisms instead of by their names. While in the *Lady Leech* the wife uses sexual metaphors to deceive her husband, here the young man uses them to break through the maiden's wall of pride and prudery. Some fabliaux use animal metaphors (*De la Pucele qui voloit voler*, MR 4:208; *Du Heron, Romania XXVI*, 85; *De la Grue*, MR 5:151; *De l'Esquiriel*, MR 5:101), while others (*De la Damoisele qui ne pooit oir parler de foutre*, MR 3:81; *De la Pucele qui abevra le polain*, MR 4:194; and ours) use elaborate sexual allegories in order to allow the protagonists to have sexual intercourse. In all cases, young girls who wish to elevate themselves, who soar in the air, so to speak, because of pride (see *The Villager and His Two Asses*), as well as those who are overly delicate and stuck-up (l. 4), are easy prey to clever young men (l. 30) who, like knight-errants, seek adventure (l. 40). Nykrog calls these maidens "the *précieuses ridicules* of the thirteenth century" (CH 69).[1]

The allegory here, once set in motion, seems to have a life of its own. It teases the imagination and is more erotic than a blunt, non-metaphorical designation of sexual organs and sexual acts.

> Here's a brand new fabliau
> That tells about a maiden so
> Extraordinarily squeamish, proud,
> Stuck-up and holier-than-thou
> That, truly (though it sounds absurd)
> Never did she hear the word
> *Fuck* or hear a dirty joke
> And not have heartburn and a stroke
> And a face like she'd been slaughtered . . .
> The father doted on his daughter.
> She was his only child. He'd do
> Anything she asked him to,

10

---

[1] The *précieuses ridicules* were seventeenth-century prudes whom the playwright Molière satyrizes.

Much more than she'd do for her father.
The two lived all alone together.
They had no servants, which was funny
Because they had a lot of money.
Now, would you like for me to tell
Why he wouldn't hire help?
Because his daughter couldn't bear
20   To have a servant, who might swear,
Or say a dirty word, or cuss.
(That's the kind of maiden she was.)
He might say *cunt* or even *prick*.
That's why the father didn't pick
A hired hand, though he did need
Someone to plow and sow the seed,
Harvest the crop, winnow and store
The grain, and do the other chores.
She said she wouldn't have one: "Never!"
30   It happened that a young man, clever,
And with a talent for deceiving
Came around looking for a living
And heard the country people's chatter
About the farmer and his daughter,
How she particularly hated
Men, and she abominated
The things men do, the things men say.
The young man's name, by the way
Was David; through the land he'd gone
40   Seeking adventure, all alone,
As brave men should. When he heard tell
About the haughty demoiselle,
Known more for fainting than for charm,
At once he hurried to the farm
Where father, daughter, and no other
Person lived, no sister, no brother,
None fit and healthy, and none lame,
Or deaf or dumb. The young man came
And found the farmer near the house,
50   Feeding the pigs, tending the cows,
Moving the woodpile to the sun—
All chores that needed to be done.
He asked him for a place to stay.
The farmer didn't turn him away
But didn't say, "Come on in," either.
He simply stood there for a breather,
Then asked, "Who are you? What's your trade?"

—"David," he answered him, and said,
"I'm looking for an honest, good
60   Employer in the neighborhood,
If there are any. I can plow
And sow and winnow. I know how
To do the things young men should do."
—"By Saint Alose, I'd hire you,
Except for one disturbing matter:
I have a proud, standoffish daughter.
Men embarrass her and vex
Her when she hears them talking sex.
I've never had a worker stay
70   Three days, before she'd hear him say
Fuck and she'd have a heart attack
And fall over on her back
As if she were about to die—
And so he'd have to go. That's why
I do the plowing, sowing, tilling.
I don't want some worker killing
My daughter with his dirty talk."
David winced and shouted, "Awk!"
And spat and got his handkerchief,
80   Wiped it across his mouth as if
He'd swallowed a fly: "Stop, my lord,
Don't say that disgusting word!
By God and by St. Astrophel,
Words like that come straight from Hell.
Don't say that word when I'm around.
I wouldn't take a hundred pounds
Sterling to stand where someone spoke
That word or told a dirty joke—
The chest pains almost knock me dead."
90   The daughter heard what David said,
And out into the yard she rushed,
Saying, "Father, Father, you must
Hire this young man. He'll do.
He'll satisfy both me and you.
He and I are kindred souls.
Sir, by the love a father owes,
I beg you, hire him. I order!"
—"Yes, of course, my darling daughter."
The farmer said, whose wits were dim,
100 They hired him and treated him
Like kinfolk risen from the dead.
     Night fell. Soon it was time for bed.

The farmer called the maiden near.
"Tell me," he asked her, "daughter, dear,
Where you think David ought to sleep."
—"If you don't mind, sir, I'll just keep
Him in my bedroom next to me.
David's trustworthy, you can see.
It's plain that he's been brought up right."
110   —"Whatever arrangements for the night
Satisfy you," the farmer said,
"Are fine with me." He made his bed
And soon was sleeping by the fire.
        Meanwhile the man that he had hired
Entered the young lady's room
To sleep by her, who in the bloom
Of beauty was so white and fair
No hawthorn flower could compare
With her fair flesh. If kings had seen
120   Her next to daughters of a queen,
They would have judged her loveliest.
        He put his hand upon her breast
And asked, "What's this?" —She answered, "These
Are my sweet breasts, white as cream cheese,
Where nothing dirty can be found."
David's hand moved further down
Her belly to the hole a woman
Has where a lover's prick can come in.
He moved his hand around and found
130   Soft, silky hair upon a mound,
Then ran his fingers through the fuzz
And sweetly asked her what it was.
—"That's my meadow," said the maiden,
"David, that you have your hand in,
Although the field is not in flower."
—"Then what you need's a flower grower
To sow fresh flowers in your field.
What's this soft furrow that I feel
In the middle of your meadow?"
140   — "That!" the farmer's daughter said, "Oh,
My fountain, which does not stick out."
—"Uh huh," said David, "what about
This little hole tucked way back here?"
—"That's my trusty trumpeteer,
Who always guards my fountain from
Any animals who come
To quench their thirst at its clear water.

He toots his trumpet," said the daughter,
"And off they scramble, seized by fear."
150   —"That's a hell of a trumpeteer,"
Said David, "And his methods stink,
Depriving animals of drink
For fear they'll trample on the grass."
—"All right, David," said the lass,
"You've had your turn at touching me.
Now what have you got? Let me see."
Then the farmer's daughter put
Her right hand, long and delicate,
On David, and went fingering
160   Up and down his everything.
She seized his penis in her fist.
"David," she said to him, "what's this?
So big and strong and stiff and thick
That you could batter down a brick
Building with it, Lord have mercy!"
—"Miss," he answered, "that's my horsey.
It's hale and hardy, proud and mighty,
But hasn't had a bite since Friday."
Her hand moved further down and found
170   A pair of balls, shaggy and round,
To wiggle in her hand and wag.
—"David," she asked, "what's in this bag?
Pin cushions? No! They're heavy. Boulders?"
—"Lady, those are my two soldiers
Who guard my horse when he trespasses
And feeds in other people's grasses.
Guarding him is their career."
—"David, let him pasture here!
Your lovely horse, your handsome prancer,
180   Here in my meadow," the maiden answered.
David rolled over. On her thick
Pubic hair he placed his prick
And said to her, beneath him lying,
"Maiden, sweet maid, my horse is dying
From thirst. His throat is parched. He's panting."
—"Then let him water at my fountain!
Come on, there's not a thing to fear!"
—"But what about the trumpeteer
Who scares the beasts who come to drink?"
190   —"Just let him try to raise a stink!"
She answered, "while your horse is drinking:
Your troops will beat him up!" —"Good thinking!"

He answered her: "good, good," and quick—
Into her cunt he put his prick
And did her wish and did her will,
And she cried out for more until
He'd done it four more times by morning.
And if the trumpet blew a warning,
The soldiers beat it blow for blow.
200   With that I end the fabliau.

XIV *William of the Falcon*

This fabliau illustrates difficulties of identity: the characters have difficulties in expressing their personal feelings and in articulating concepts. Verbal communication between two individuals is not effective, and the tale itself is in danger of never reaching a conclusion — saved from its impasse only by a timely metamorphosis into a fabliau. The tale also suffers from an identity crisis. The most dramatic scene is the one in which all three characters are present (ll. 471–527). It holds in suspense the outcome and the nature of the tale: a quick, reasonable, or a tragic resolution here, and the tale would not have been a fabliau. Suddenly, the tale shifts to a fabliau: the husband, frustrated by his exclusion from the apparent communication, goes into a rage, threatens to beat his wife (ll. 515–21), and apparently makes a move to do so (l. 520), if he is not told about what is going on. As soon as his wife mentions that William has come to see her in her room, the husband is transformed into the stereotyped jealous and brutal husband of the fabliaux. The author must have realized that the only way of bringing his narrative to a conclusion was to end it as a fabliau.

As Bédier judiciously notes (B 364, 365), the separation between the two sides of the medieval literary coin — the fabliau and Renart on one side and the Round Table on the other—is indeed thin. Our fabliau stands as an admirable connector.

> Whoever wishes to repeat
> A good adventure should delete
> Nothing that's worth the leaving in.
> With that in mind I shall begin.
>   Once long ago there lived a youth,
> A handsome, bright young man in truth,
> Named William. Even if you tried
> A hundred countries, far and wide,
> You'd find no better man than he.
> Though of the aristocracy,
> His knighthood he had not attained,
> But he had served a chatelain[1]
> For seven years now as a squire,

10

---

[1] Chatelain: lord of a castle.

Receiving nothing for his hire
Because he worked to win his arms.
The time it took did not alarm
The young man though, and here's the reason:
Love held him locked within a prison:
He loved his master's wife, and thus
20   Was satisfied with where he was.
He loved her so distractedly,
He had no way of getting free.
But she had no idea at all
How much she held his heart in thrall.
If she had seen into his heart,
She would have kept herself apart
Without exchanging any words.
I will not lie to you, my lords:
Women in this are much to blame.
30   When any woman knows the game
Of love is hers, the lover had,
Then she will let love drive him mad,
And never have a word to say
To him, for she would rather play
With some vile tramp, not worth a curse,
Than with a friend who's truly hers.
But if the lady even cares
A little, if she never spares
A word for him, she does not well.
40   May God condemn her soul to Hell
For the great sin that she commits.
When she has caught him in the nets
From which he cannot struggle loose,
It's surly of her to refuse
To be the one to help him out,
Since she is all he thinks about.
Now to my tale. Enough discourse.
     William put all his strength and force
In loving her. Love had control
50   And jurisdiction of his soul.
Great martyrdom he must endure.[1]
     And now I'd like to speak of her:[2]

---

[1] Martyrdom: in the courtly love tradition, where love is raised to the status of religion, William's suffering is like the suffering that a martyr endures for the faith.

[2] Lines 52-107 are typical of descriptions of beautiful women in courtly romances, particularly lines 80-97, starting at the top of the woman's head and

She was exceeding beautiful.
The wild flowers blooming on the hill,
The lily flower, the rose of May—
She was more beautiful than they.
If you had searched the whole world round,
No fairer lady could you have found
In all the lands from East to West—
60   Not even where women are loveliest,
The noble kingdom of Castile.
By subtle art I shall reveal
The riches of her loveliness.
Arrayed in jewels and perfect dress,
What joy the lady was to look on!
More lovely than the molted falcon,
Royal parrot or sparrow hawk!
Her dress was purple, and her cloak
Was stitched and starred with shining gold.
70   The ermine lining wasn't old
Or worn or frayed, but fresh and thick.
The cloak was hemmed about the neck
In white and gray with sable hide,
Neither too narrow nor too wide.
If ever yet I have portrayed
The form God gave to wife or maid,
Now may my heart receive the grace
To sketch her lovely form and face
Without their being falsified,
80   For when her hair was left untied,
It shone so bright that anyone
Who saw would swear that it was spun
From purest gold. Her forehead shone
Like finely cut and polished stone,
Her eyebrows brown and widely spread,
Her eyes were laughing in her head,
Deep and clear, gray-green and bright.
The *fleurs de lis* on field of white
Are not so aptly set in place
90   As every feature of her face
To make the work of art complete.
Her nose was slender, straight, and neat.
Her mouth was small and round and closed,

---

working downward; line 99, disclaiming ability to describe her in verse; and lines
104–6, claiming that nature has outdone herself in creating the woman.

Vermillion as the passerose;[1]
Her chin was fresh as can be thought;
Smooth as crystal was her throat.
Her breasts were round as little apples,
Firm and small with little nipples.
There's nothing more for me to say:
100 To lead men's hearts and minds astray
God made her perfect—no! much more—
Never her like was seen before.
Never was lady lovelier.
Nature gave all in making her,
And when there was no more to give,
Nature impoverished had to live.
About her beauty no more I'll say.
  The lady's husband went one day
A long way off upon a journey
110 To gain more honor at a tourney
Far away in another land.
Since he was mighty, rich, and grand,
He took along a great parade
Of knights and serving men, and stayed
For many months. No knight that went
With him was less than excellent.
The greatest coward in his party
Was unreservedly brave and hearty.
William was scared. He didn't want
120 To go to any tournament.
He much preferred to stay around
The house. The god of love had wound
Him up so tight, he didn't know
What to do or how to throw
The evil off that held him tied.
Now to himself he moaned and sighed,
"Oh God! How wretched and forlorn
I am. Alas that I was born!
I've lifted all my love to where
130 I haven't even got a prayer
Of ever getting love repaid.
I think I shouldn't have delayed
So long in telling her I love her.
If all my life I pine and suffer
Without her knowledge, I'm a fool.

---

[1] Passerose: variety of rose, also known as "rose-tremière."

I know: I'll tell her how I feel.
(I've had sufficient time to court
Every lady in every port.)
You'll tell her ... well?—You'll tell her what?
140   You must be brave—which you are not—
To let her know how you endure
Anguish and martyrdom for her.
—I'll speak to her, you mustn't doubt—
The hard part though is starting out.
I'll speak my love aloud and clearly.
Oh, what's the use! I shouldn't really!
I really don't know what to do!
When all this started, then I knew
I could retreat when the time came,
150   But love has set me all aflame."
William summoned up his nerve
And didn't hesitate or swerve,
But straight to the lady's room he rushed,
And when he reached the door, he pushed
It open wide without a sound
And came into the room and found,
By chance, the lady there alone.
Her maids in waiting had all gone
Into another room to stitch
160   A lion or leopard (I don't know which)
Upon silk cloth. They laughed and played
And had good fun. Their work displayed
The coat of arms of the lady's knight.
William didn't want to wait.
     The lady sat upon her bed.
Never had man of woman bred
Beheld a lovelier form alive.
William was worried. When would arrive
His golden opportunity?
170   William looked long and longingly
Upon her; then he said, "Hello."
The lady wasn't nervous, though.
"William," she answered, "come inside."
She sweetly laughed. But William sighed
And answered, "Yes, ma'am, willingly."
—"My dear friend, come and sit by me."
But little did she apprehend
How much her greeting, "My dear friend,"
Had set the young man's heart aflutter.
180   Nothing could have made her utter

Such words of friendship had she known.
Her face was beautiful. It shone
As William sat there on her bed.
They laughed and joked, and much they said
On many subjects far and wide.
William took a breath and sighed:
"Lady, I beg of you, pay heed
To what I ask of you. I need
Your counsel. Tell me what you'd say...."
190   —"Of course I'll give it. Ask away."
—"If clerk, or knight of high degree,
Or someone from the bourgeoisie
Should fall in love—or even a squire—
With lowly woman, or with higher,
With duchess, dame or demoiselle,
Fine lady or young mademoiselle
Of any station or degree,
What would your opinion be
If he has loved her seven years
200   And kept it hidden and he fears
Still to tell her anything—
What martyrdom he's suffering—
And yet he still could tell his love
If only he were brave enough
And the occasion would appear
To open up his heart to her,
And what I really wish I knew
Is what you think he ought to do
And whether he does right or wrong
210   To keep his love from her so long."
The lady answered, "Listen, William,
Here's my advice. Here's what I'd tell him.
I don't believe he's very smart
Not to tell her from his heart
How much he loves her, since he can.
She'd have to pity the poor man.
It would be very foolish of her
Not to accept the love he's offered
And one day wish to God she had.
220   But since Love rules and drives him mad
And willy-nilly pulls him along,
Then he should speak. He must be strong
And tell his love. That's what I'd urge.
He loves her, yes, but love takes courage.
This principle must be observed:

The god of love cannot be served
By cowards. Lovers must be brave,
Since they are bound to be Love's slave.
By Paul, if I were in his place,
230   I'd tell the lady face to face,
And she would have to hear me, too.
And that's what this man ought to do,
And let her love him if she will."
     William looked a little ill
And moaned and sighed and then began:
"Lady," he said, "behold the man,
The one who long, without relief,
For love of you has suffered grief.
Lady, I didn't dare to tell
240   The martyrdom and bitter hell
I've had to bear these seven years,
And telling it, I'm filled with fears.
Lady, I give myself to you.
Do with me what you want to do.
I am your serving man and slave.
Sweet lady, heal this wound I have
Inside my body, deep and raw.
There isn't anyone at all
Who can restore me to my health,
250   But you. I boast of this myself.
All yours I am, was, will remain.
In greater agony or pain
No man has ever had to live.
Lady, I'm asking you to give
Your love to me, the love whose lack
Has put my body on the rack."
     And now the lady fully grasped
What it was that William asked,
But not a coin or a crust of bread
260   Would she have given for what he said.
The lady looked at him and spoke.
"William," she asked, "is this a joke?
I wouldn't love you for the world.
Go play your jokes on some poor girl.
No one has ever dared to play
Such jokes on me before today.
But one thing's sure. By God I vow
If you should speak as you spoke now
To me again, I'll have you shamed.
270   I didn't know your love was aimed

At me. What are you asking for?
You've got your nerve. Go! There's the door!
Get out of here, get off this place.
Don't you ever show your face
Anywhere within my sight.
Your little offer will delight
My husband when he finds it out.
When he comes home, you needn't doubt,
I'll tell my husband word for word
280 The whole, long sermon I've endured.
I think you are an imbecile.
Whoever was responsible
For bringing you here should be drowned.
Get out, young man! Don't stick around!"
When William realized what she said,
He was amazed and half struck dead.
Much he repented having come.
He stood there, stupified and dumb,
Downhearted, mortified, dismayed.
290 "Alas," he thought, "I am betrayed."
    Messengers, who always lose
Their welcome when they bring bad news,
Are what young William reminds me of.
But still he was compelled by love,
Still felt the need to speak to her
And not leave matters as they were.
"Lady," he said, "I'm sorely grieved
That this is all I have received
From you. But lady, you have sinned.
300 You have me trapped and tied and pinned
And treat me worse. You want my death—
Kill me and get it over with.
Listen, I asked you for your love.
I beg a gift, and I will prove
My need for it. I will not eat
Until the day that you see fit."
The lady answered, "By the mass,
You're really going to have to fast
To get my love. You will not eat
310 Before the sowing of the wheat."
    Then William rose and went away
Without good-bye, without good day,
Arranged his bed and went to bed.
But little rest did William get.
He stayed in bed three days complete

And nothing did he drink or eat,
And on the fourth he still was there,
And still the lady didn't spare
A look at him when she went past.
320   But William did know how to fast.
He wouldn't even eat a crust.
The sickness in him would not rest.
It nagged and worried him night and day.
He lost his color, pined away.
No wonder he was losing weight:
Three days, he never slept or ate!
William lay in bed and shook,
And when he rolled his eye to look,
The lovely lady, full of charms—
330   He thought he felt her in his arms,
Lying there with him and granting
Everything that he was wanting.
And while this lasted, it was bliss
To hold her, trading kiss for kiss.
And when at last the vision waned,
He trembled, sighed, reached out his hand,
But air was all that he embraced.
Foolishness is what fools chase!
He searched for her throughout the bed.
340   She wasn't there. He beat his head,
His face and chest, and tore his hair.
Love held him tied. Love was the snare.
Love held him hurt in chains of steel.
He wanted her to be there still.
The vision should have stayed forever,
But nothing else but chills and fever
The god of loving would allow.
     I'll speak about the husband now,
Riding from the tournament
350   With many men at arms. He sent
A messenger to his chateau
To find his wife and let her know
The day her lord was coming home.
Fifteen prisoners came with him,
All of them rich and wealthy knights,
And many other spoils besides.
The message of this messenger
Was joyous, welcome news to her.
Delighted, she made sure that all
360   Was ready in the banquet hall

To wine and dine the many guests.
Everything must look the best
For the arrival of her lord.
As for William, he was scared.
The lady thought she ought to tell
William that her lord was well
And coming from the tournament,
And ask him what on earth he meant
Not touching any of his food.
370   She came beside his bed and stood.
A good long while she waited there,
But William didn't notice her.
"William," she called at last, "Hello!"
He didn't answer yes or no.
His mind was somewhere in a cloud.
This time she called his name quite loud
And with her finger poked his head.
When William heard, he jerked in bed.
And when he felt, he broke out sweating.
380   He saw her, and he shouted greeting:
"Lady, welcome! Thank God you're here!
You've come to bring me health and cheer.
Please for the sake of God almighty,
Lady, I beg you, show some pity."
She answered, "By the faith I owe you,
William, no pity will I show you,
Not the kind you're asking for.
Is this the way you thank my lord
For all the kindness he has done?
390   Wooing his wife when he is gone?
You love him too. Is that the way
You love? You'll never see the day
You manage me or make me love you.
William, it's very foolish of you
To keep from eating night and day.
You know, you'll kill yourself that way.
Your soul will perish if you do,
For I will never give to you
The gift you keep on asking for.
400   Get up! Get out of bed! My lord
Is riding homeward from the tourney.
I cannot tell how long the journey,
But when he comes and finds you there,
Lying in bed, by God, I swear,
He'll learn from me what the reason is.

You'll never get away with this."
—"It won't be any use," he said,
"To slice my arms and legs and head,
Because I'll never eat, I swear.
410   Lady, around my neck I wear
A heavy weight that will not fall.
I can't defend myself at all
Against you, though I fast and die.
Tell him the truth; I won't deny."
At that the lady turned and went
With no love promised and none meant.
She came to where the dining hall
Was decorated wall to wall.
The tables all were set in place
420   With tablecloths of white cut lace
And loaded with good things to eat:
Bread and wine and skewered meat.
    At last the knights came riding in,
And now the feasting could begin.
More men were served and eating well
Than this short narrative could tell.
Lady and lord together ate.
The husband looked up from his plate
To see if William would be there
430   To stand and serve behind his chair,
But he was nowhere to be seen.
He wondered where he could have been
And turned to her and said, "My dear,
I cannot see young William here.
I pray you, can you tell me why?"
—"Lately William's been too shy,"
The lady said, "But I'll explain
What's going on. The simple, plain
And honest truth is this: he's ill.
440   And there will never be a pill
To cure the sickness William has."
Her husband answered, "By the mass,
I'm sorry he's not feeling good."
But if the lord had understood
The reason he was feeling bad,
William would have died in bed,
(So far, he doesn't understand.
But death and danger are at hand.
He'll find out soon. If William still
450   Refuses food, I'm sure she'll tell

What sickness keeps him in his bed.
And William will have to lose his head.)
    The knights got up from empty plates.
The lady didn't want to wait.
She took her husband by the sleeve:
"My Lord, I'm shocked. I can't believe
You've not seen William yet. You ought
To visit him and find out what
His ailment is and why he's ailing.
460   Day by day the boy is failing."
They went together to the room
And found him pensive, full of gloom,
But unaffected by the fear
Of death, which surely must be near.
He'd had enough of pain and grief
And hoped his dying would be brief.
The lord knelt down beside the bed
At William's feet and bowed his head,
And like an honest man and good,
470   Reasoned with him as best he could.
"William, my dear young friend," he said,
"What sickness keeps you locked in bed?
Tell me what's wrong. I'll help you gladly."
—"My Lord," he said, "I'm doing badly.
The sickness runs from head to toes.
In sudden fits it comes and goes.
Every limb is racked with pain.
I don't think I'll get up again."
—"Well, won't you eat or take some water?"
480   —"No food or drink. It doesn't matter.
Nothing God made could suit my diet."
The lady couldn't have kept quiet
If she had choked on every word:
"By God, we're wasting time, my lord!
William may speak the way he wishes,
But I know what the truth of this is—
What the causes, where they linger.
The sickness isn't in his finger!
This sickness makes the victim sweat,
490   Tremble in his bed and fret."
She looked at William in the eye:
"So help me God, I will not lie.
William, unless you break your fast,
The hour has come around at last
When all your eating days are over."

But William only answered, "Never.
You have the power. You give the word.
You are my lady, he my lord,
But though you sliced my hands and feet,
500   Even then I would not eat."
The lady cried, "Now hear the truth,
My lord, about this foolish youth!
When you rode to the tournament,
William, who's lying sick here, went
Into my room to visit me."
—"What? Lady! Into your room, did he?
What on earth did he do that for?
Why did he enter your chamber door!"
—"I'll tell you sir. He came and stood—
510   William, will you have some food?
My husband's going to hear the shame
And gross dishonor to his name."
—"No!" shouted William, "By Saint Pete,
Never! I will never eat!"
The lord said, "Lady, you will make
A fool of me if I don't take
This heavy stick I have in hand
And beat you till you cannot stand
And bruise your sides and back and head!"
520   —"Wait, my lord. Hold on!" she said,
"I'm going to tell you everything—
William! are you listening?
Now will you eat? I'm telling him."
But William didn't move a limb.
He heaved a sigh most pitiful:
"Never will I eat until
This nagging heartache is assuaged."
At last the lady's anger changed
To pity, and "My lord," she said,
530   "This William, whom you see in bed,
Asked me for your—falcon, sir,
And I refused, you may be sure,
Because I'm very much aware
Your birds, my lord, are your affair."
The lord said, "This was badly done.
I'd rather all the birds I own—
Falcon, peregrine, and hawk—
Were dead than William on his back
And hungry even for a day."
540   The wife deceived her lord that way.

"Then give it to him," she replied,
"If that will keep you satisfied.
I'm not the one to tell him no.
William, by the faith I owe,
My lord and husband has agreed,
And it would be an evil deed
If I continued to refuse."
William, when he heard this news,
Almost burst from joy and pleasure.
His happiness could know no measure.
Soon he was up and soon was dressed,
His sickness gone. No more distressed,
He put his socks and his shoes on
And straight to the lady's room was gone.
And when the lady saw him come,
She breathed a sigh and gazed on him.
Love had pierced her to the heart,
And now she had to have her part.
Love chilled and burned her with the fever.
Love made her pale and blush and shiver.
"William, young man," the master said,
"You must have really lost your head
To crave my hawk so desperately.
Letting her go is hard for me.
There's no one else, not mad or sane,
No prince or count or noble thane
With prayers or service who could hope
To make me give my falcon up."
The knight gave orders to his men
To bring the falcon to him then.
They brought it quickly, and the lord
Took the jess and gave the bird
To William, who accepted it
With thanks and pleasure, as was fit.
　　The wife said, "Now you have your falcon.
Two half crowns are a crown, I reckon."
And she was right: one thing—two words.
One word would get him two rewards,
For by next morning, he had more:
The falcon which he hungered for,
And from the lady, joy more sweet
Than pear or plum is good to eat.
　　This fabliau is one more proof
That I am giving of a truth
For all young men who ever went

550

560

570

580

Tilting in Love's tournament:
When they have given up their heart
To a lovely lady, they must start
Immediately, and they must dare
590   To press their love with pleas and prayer,
And if at first she answers no,
He must press on and not let go.
No matter who he is, if often
And stubbornly he prays, she'll soften;
For that's how William wooed the lady,
With all his heart and soul and body
And took great joy as his reward
For all his pains, as you have heard.
And may God give great joy today
600   Without postponement or delay
To those who, serving Love, must bear
Sorrow, anguish, and despair,
And I will also, when the lover
Keeps courage. Now this tale is over.

XV   *The Lai of Aristotle*

HENRI D'ANDELI

The lai is sometimes referred to as *Alexander and Aristotle*. Aristotle (484–322 B.C.) was the most admired philosopher of the middle ages from the thirteenth century on. Alexander the Great (356–323 B.C.), along with Charlemagne and Arthur, was one of the great hero kings of medieval literature. Although a great deal of false and questionable legend had grown up around him, it is true that in 343 B.C. Aristotle was appointed by King Philip of Macedonia to serve as tutor to Philip's son, Alexander, and during his conquest of Asia, Alexander did indeed marry Roxana, a Persian princess from what is now northwestern Afganistan. Aristotle, however, did not accompany the young king on his conquest of Asia, although Alexander sent back information and biological specimens to him.

This tale has been thought too elegant, too courtly, too refined to be a fabliau. It is, in fact, a seduction tale in which the language, sentiments, and actions conform to courtly regulations. In his long introduction, its author, Henri d'Andeli, a cleric and university intellectual, seems to reproach the fabliaux for their crude expression but not for their pleasant plots. Like the author of *William of the Falcon*, he dramatizes mental conflicts and, like many other fableors, the triumph of sexuality over philosophy. Underlying those conflicts, however, is the danger of emotions which impair the reason. This warning seems to place our lai very much within the ranks of the fabliaux.

Henri, a respected author of several intellectual and allegorical works including the *Bataille des sept Arts*, attempts to distance himself from vulgar jongleurs (ll. 38–59). The fact that he tried his hand at composing a fabliau shows that the genre was not considered an unworthy one in his time.

> Someone who can speak fine words
> Should not hold back, but make them heard.
> And one should listen to fine speech,
> Because when heeded it can teach
> Wisdom and the courtesies.
> Good words are always bound to please
> Good people. That's the custom here.
> All bad people do is sneer
> Whenever they hear noble phrases.

10   Whereas an honest person praises
      All that is decent and well spoken,
      A slanderer, by the same token,
      Despises what he can't degrade.
      Envy is his toil and trade.
      Envy dwells inside his spirit.
      Praise someone else? He will not hear it.
      When someone's praised, he takes offense
      And contradicts the compliments.
      But why should good make people mad?
20   Ill-bred people, low and bad,
      What does it get you when you stack
      Your own faults on another's back?
      In truth, there's no excuse for it.
      Mortal sin's what you commit
      Twice; one sin's slander and the other
      Is your dishonesty; you cover
      The dirt you do with dirt you speak.
      That's the behavior of a sneak,
      Whose envy never ceases swelling.
30   There isn't any point in dwelling
      Upon this subject. I don't see
      What further profit there could be
      In criticizing these cruel drones
      (Let's just call them Ganelons)[1]
      Because they couldn't hold their peace
      Even if they were deceased,
      They're so in love with their vocation.
            And now back to the recitation
      Of the adventure I've begun.
40   The subject seemed a worthy one
      When I first heard it, one that ought
      To be with skillful rhyming wrought,
      Delivered in a language free
      From all that smacks of vulgarity,
      Because scurrility and dirt
      Don't have any place at court.
      Never will filth and dirt and grime
      Be the subject of my rhyme.
      I never have and never shall

---

[1] Ganelon's betrayal of Charlemagne's greatest knight, Roland, is depicted in the 11th century epic, *Chanson de Roland*. By the 13th century, the word *Ganelon* was synonymous with *traitor*.

50 And never do let crude words foul
My way of speaking or my poems,
Because improper speech deforms,
Maims, disfigures, spoils the flavor
Of all it touches. I shall never
Be caught composing vulgar drivel.
Vulgarity and trash mean trouble.
Instead, I'll tell, in rhyme and measure,
For your profit and your pleasure
A tale worth spice and fruit and cheese.
60   We find that the great king of Greece,
Alexander, made himself lord
Over all other kings and poured
His wrath upon them. Casting them down,
He rose and grew and gained renown.
Largesse, the god, who was his mother,
Loaded him with success. She covers
Misers with shames and bitternesses.
Those who are generous she blesses.
The more the stinginess, the less
70 The generosity from Largesse.
Gold never governed Alexander.
His knights were his treasure. He made them grander
Than gold—unlike most other princes!
Your average prince scrapes, scrimps and chintzes
And hides his money in a hole;
Honor and good are not his goal.
But Alexander gathered tribute,
Which he delighted to distribute.
He took, held, gave all. Alexander
80 Gave himself up with wild abandon
To Largesse. Thus he gained great glory.
     And now I'll get back to my story.
When Greece and Egypt's monarch put
Great India beneath his foot
A second time, he had to tarry
A while in his new territory.
And if you're interested in knowing
Why he took so long in going
But stayed instead, and didn't try
90 To get away from there, here's why:
Love, the Emperor, who spares
No one when he sets his snares,
Had chained and tamed him, soul and limb,
And made a lover out of him.

He didn't chafe at being chained,
Because the mistress he had gained
Was lovelier than he could ask.
He didn't care for any task
Except to love and be with her.
100 Love is a mighty conqueror
Indeed when even he who wields
Most power in the great world yields
To love, forgets and humbles himself
And cares for only someone else.
But this is reasonable, for such is
Love's nature: any man Love clutches
Will not put up a struggle. Love
Rules as tyrannically above
A monarch as above the poorest
110 Beggar in France's fields and forests,
For absolute is Love's dominion.
        Thus Alexander and his Indian
Dallied day after day. And people
Were talking: "All he does is sleep all
The morning and neglect to rule,
Fritter his life and play the fool.
He won't budge from his courtesan:
Frankly, I don't think he can!"
True. He could not. For Love required
120 His service. So did she. She fired
His flesh and pricked it with Love's spurs
Until his will was thrall to hers.
But she was just as much a victim,
Because however hard she pricked him,
He worked Love's will with her as well.
Who was the winner? Hard to tell.
She knew Love's art, each sly manoeuver,
But now she'd fallen for her lover.
No wonder that he stayed until
130 People complained. He let his will
Rule over him. He had no say.
Obey his will or disobey
The Law of Love: there is no other
Choice open to a courtly lover.
"The king's behavior's a disgrace,"
His own men said, not to his face.
But when his tutor, Aristotle,
The great professor, heard the tattle,
He knew his duty: to reprove

140   The king in private counsel: "You've
Abandoned your barons, and for what?
A foreign woman!" The king said, "But
What do you want from me? I think
These gossipers who say I shrink
From duty never loved at all.
Love just one woman: that's Love's law.
Please her alone: that's Love's command.
Any critic who can't stand
For men to go where their hearts guide
150   Hasn't any love inside."
But Aristotle, who knew all
The knowledge learned since Adam's fall,
Reasoned, remonstrated, and taught
The king of Greece that he had brought
Shame on himself. What? To linger
Beside that foreign woman longer
Than a week and never pay the least
Attention to his knights—no feast
For them, no honor, no respect....
160   "And that's the duty you neglect,
King," said Alexander's master;
"Now they could put you out to pasture
Like a beast to graze and drink from puddles.
Your wits were too much in a muddle
When under a foreign girl's influence
Your heart and body strayed like truants
From moderation's level track.
I beg and order you: turn back
To your old self—no hesitation.
170   You're paying for your dissipation."
    So Alexander kept away
Many a long hour and long day
From her because of the insistence
Of his professor. He kept his distance
Submissively, but let me stress
The young king's will had not grown less.
He walked the well-worn path to her door
No more. And yet he loved her more
Than ever, more than when they'd kept
180   Close company. But now he checked
His will for fear of doing wrong
And stopped his visits, but he clung
To memories, would not erase
The image of her form and face,

Her crystal forehead.... Love kept fresh
The thought of her unblemished flesh,
Her cherry lips and her blonde hair:
"To melancholy, bleak despair,
Everyone condemns my life.
190   My tutor sets my mind at strife
Against the thing my heart requires.
Other wills, others' desires
Hem me in: I'm losing my wits!
Witless I am when I permit
Other wills to waste my mind.
My master and my men combined
Don't feel a tenth of what I feel.
If they define what's right and real
For me, all that I have I lose.
200   Can Love live by a list of do's
And don't's? No! Love must rule the lover!"
Alexander thought things over
Till back he rushed to the one who could
Give him delight, make his life good.
She leapt up when she saw the king.
She had been sitting, sorrowing
Because her lover wasn't there.
"My lord," she said, "I am aware
Of how much anguish you must suffer.
210   Tell me, how does a courtly lover,
When he loves something, manage keeping
From it?" Then she started weeping
And said no more.
                              "My dear sweetheart,"
Said Alexander, "let me start
By saying this: I had a reason
For shunning you so long a season:
My knights and lords said it's a crime
For me dissipate my time
With you, not them. And when my guide
220   And tutor heard, he took their side,
Blamed me, and gave me a good scolding,
But I've been acting wrong in holding
Back where the will of Love directed
Because my philosopher objected.
I didn't want to risk more shame."
—"Aha! So that's who is to blame,"
She said, "but this I swear, by damn,
I'm not the strategist I am

If I don't get comeuppance fast.
230   Soon you'll be able to lambaste
And put to shame that mean old boorish
White-haired philosopher of yours.
If I live twenty-four more hours
And Love stands by me, Love, whose powers
Never have failed, your tutor's wisdom,
Grammar, science and syllogism
Won't avail when we cross swords.
Nature will win. In other words,
If you get up tomorrow morning
240   Early, you'll find your teacher learning
A lesson. Nature will unschool
Your scholar of scholarship and rules
For logic, law, and thinking straight.
He'll get a switching his white pate
Won't soon forget. This scholar never
Had such cruel switching or so clever
As when tomorrow I step into
The garden underneath his window.
He'll eat his insults. Sire, install
250   Yourself behind the tower wall
And watch the fun. I'll do my part."
        When she said this, the king took heart.
He put her head upon his shoulder
And kissed her, saying, "My brave soldier,
If I love anyone but you,
May God have nothing more to do
With me. Nothing I could have wished
Is lacking from your love." They kissed
Goodbye. She stayed. He went away.
260   Early, when other people lay
In bed, she rose. Let them sleep on:
She didn't mind getting up at dawn.
She stepped beneath the tower wall,
Wearing a chemise, that's all:
A dotted indigo dressing gown.
It was a pleasant day in June,
The garden blooming, green and gold.
She had no fear of catching cold
Because of summer in the air.
270   Nature had gardened her with care:
Lilies and roses in her face
Were blooming. Not a trace
Of imperfection marred her simple

Elegance. She wore no wimple,
Ribbons, or headband. Her long, unbound
Ringlets were all the gold that crowned
Her head. Praise God they were not shorn!
She whom Nature had adorned
Barefoot through the orchard traipsed
280   Without a belt about her waist,
Lifting her skirts as she walked along,
Softly singing this little song:
        From the olive orchard, singing,
        See my lady come to me.
        The gladiola's springing
        Beneath the alder tree,
        And the fountains wash the air.
        See her golden hair!
        I see her, see her, see her, see!
290   *And give myself to her.*
And when the king, who up above
Leaned from a window to hear his love
Begin her song, heard her begin,
What ecstasy she threw him in
With words and music.
                            Hearing her,
At a low window, the philosopher,
Will learn how to expatiate
On how, when forces separate
Lovers, they strive to come together.
300   From this day forward, he will never
Scold Alexander for a sin
Discovered to exist in him,
Himself, the time he voluntarily
Got drunk on love. He'd got up early
To read his books, but when he saw
Her walking back and forth below,
An old memory in his heart stirred,
And he closed his books: he moaned, "Oh Lord,
Draw this miracle closer still,
310   And I'll surrender mind and will—
To what? Love? Me surrender?
What am I saying? Never. Never
Have I, who always was so smart,
Acted so dumb. I've lost my heart.
One little look, and Love moves in;
Honor, out. Shame and chagrin
Are all this service earns. I'm old,

Wrinkled, white-headed, almost bald,
Splotched and pale, ugly, scrawny,
320 And a philosopher. I'm brainy.
Years of uninterrupted study
That taught me more than anybody—
All wasted! I've got a lot to learn.
But Love unlearns me to intern
Me in his school, where Love has stuck
Many a good man to instruct
By disinstructing. Love destroys
Knowledge to teach. I'm Love's school boy
And captive. Therefore, since I'm caught,
330 I must give in. Law, move out,
Don't stay just for politeness' sake.
Welcome to my heart, Love; make
Yourself at home, since anyway
There's nothing I can do. Come; stay."
As Aristotle wracked his mind,
The lady found some flowers to bind
Around some sprigs of mint for garlands,
And as he watched her walk along,
She thought of love and sang this song:
340   *I'm always caught in romance.*
        "Pretty girl there washing shirts,
        I love you so much it hurts."
        I'm always caught in romance
        Wherever I happen to glance.
About the orchard the lady lingered,
And the philosopher was angered
She wasn't coming close enough.
The lady really knew her stuff
And had him lured and held and tethered.
350 She chose a beautifully feathered
Arrow. She had planned this well.
Now it would be an easy kill.
She wove into her golden hair
The wreath of flowers, taking care
To make him think she thought no one
Was looking at her as she spun
Her spell and wrapped him in her power.
She wandered nearer to the tower,
Singing a weavers' song, to hold
360 Her quarry so it wouldn't bolt:
        Beneath the orchard where the pears are growing
        Beside the fountain's crystal water flowing,

The daughter of the king is softly sighing:
"Ah, Count Walter!
Your love has taken away my laughter."
She laughed and sang. But when she walked
Past the low window where he gawked,
He reached and seized her shoulder strap.
He couldn't help it; he was trapped
370   Inside his flesh. Flesh moved his will.
At that, the old cat's candle spilled
And sputtered out upon the floor.
He's a goner. That's for sure.
The lady turned around and gasped,
"What's going on? Lord, help! Who grasped
My shoulder? Eek! Unhand me, sir."
—"Lady," said the philosopher
(Who now could teach a course on folly)
"Welcome to my window." —"Golly,
380   Sir," she said, "is this you here?"
—"It is I," he answered, "my dear, dear
Lady. For your sake I'd pawn
Soul, body, honor, all I own.
Love and nature have me so
Reconstructed I can't let go."
—"Well, then," she answered, "since it's love,
I wouldn't want to put you off,
But people have been acting oddly.
I don't know what busybody
390   Has told the king that spending time
Away from court with me's a crime."
—"Tut," said the teacher, "let's not speak
Of that. No fear. I'll oil his squeak.
I'll put a stop to all the blabbing,
Babbling, squabbling, and backstabbing.
I've got the king in the palm of my hand.
He fears me more than any man,
But now for God's sake, come inside
And stay until you've gratified
400   Me with your polished flesh and skin."
—"Well, sir," she said, "before you win
Me over to foolishness, there's one
Little favor I'd like done
If you don't mind, since you're so smitten:
I won't be ready till I've ridden
All around this little track
Of grassy orchard horsey-back

On you. And, Master Aristotle,
You really ought to wear a saddle,
410   So my procession will be more
Decorous, don't you think?" —"Sure,"
Aristotle said he'd do
Anything she asked him to.
(His old back, when it bears the saddle,
Will prove that Love has won the battle
And made an ass of the great man.)
Without another word, she ran
To saddle up and cinch his tummy.
Love turns a genius to a dummy
420   When nature summons him, because
The smartest clerk who ever was
Put on a saddle for a horse
And pranced and cantered on all fours
Over the grass like a skittish sorrel.
(I tell this story for the moral;
Be patient and await the point.)
He trotted up and let her mount
Upon his back. Across the green
He happily bounced the lady, seen
430   By anyone who wished to witness,
Carefree as a colt, and witless,
Because his wits were lost to Love.
The lady gaily rode above
The master, whom she spurred along,
Laughing as she sang a song
In a voice that was lovely, rich, and full.
    This is the way that lovers go,
    (Beautiful Jill is washing wool.)
    Doctor Donkey, I'm on to you.
440   *This is the way that lovers go,*
    And donkeys that lovers ride on, too.
When Alexander, from his tower,
Saw the whole trick, for all his power,
Wealth, and land from there to Athens,
He couldn't have kept himself from laughing.
"Well, Professor Aristotle,"
He cried, "I see you have to trot all
Over the grass. What! Have you bidden
Goodbye to your senses? Being ridden
450   Like a dumb beast? The other day
You gave me orders: stay away
From her. Now *you're* down on the grass

With no more reason than an ass,
Ridden, driven, pasture fed!"
      Aristotle raised his head,
And the lady got down off.
Then meekly, with a little cough,
He answered, "Sire, I'm in the wrong,
But my mistake proves all along
460   I was right to fear for you,
Whose juices still run burning through
Your young body, since I, though old
And wise when Love struck, couldn't hold
Fast and I fell to the position
You saw me in. My disquisitions,
Systems and science and learning!—Nature,
Who tames and taxes every creature,
In one short hour wiped them out.
Conclude, therefore, without a doubt:
470   If I play such a public fool,
Despite my well-known wisdom, you'll
Be lucky to get off unscathed."
      That's how Aristotle saved
Some dignity on which to stand.
She had accomplished all she'd planned;
The king applauded her revenge
Against the man who drove a wedge
Of words between himself and her,
But now the old philosopher
480   Talked his way from the trap she'd laid him
So well that laughing he forgave him.
But Aristotle did not still
Command the king to check his will,
Since that commandment lacked conviction.
      Now I'd like to pose a question.
My source is Cato, who excelled
In writing wisely, living well,
And what he says concerns the story
I'm telling: *Turpe est doctori*
490   *Cum culpa se redarguit.*[1]
And here's what Cato means by it:
Anybody who is caught
Doing what he says others ought

---

[1] "The teacher is shamed when his guilt contradicts him." A quote from the *Disticha Catonis* (see Delbouille, *Le Lai d'Aristote*, 104).

Not to do receives the blame
His folly merits, and his claim
To be a teacher loses credit.
Truly, Aristotle said it
Was folly for the king to love;
Then Aristotle let Love shove
500   Himself into the worst positions
And didn't make the least resistance.
But mustn't we excuse him, too,
For doing what he had to do?
Of course we must, for Love, which forces
All men and women with remorseless
Power to obey its will
Forced him. Therefore we shouldn't grill
The teacher for what Nature bade.
It's not his fault. He just obeyed.
510   He didn't *study* being silly.
      By this tale, Henry of Andeli
Proves you can't demoralize
True lovers long. And you can't prise
Their will from them, for Love alone
Can make a lover's will its own
And torture him the way it pleases.
Whoever won't accept this thesis
Is no true lover. Love's too bitter
For him. And yet there is no better
520   Means of holding to love than this:
Tasting all its bitterness.
Therefore, an unhappy lover
Ought to be glad to have to suffer:
For every bad thing, twenty best things
Come to those who keep on testing
Their loves, since Love will turn about
And bless the lovers who hold out
Patiently through martyrdom,
For after hardship, pleasures come.
530   This poem is spoken for a moral:
People shouldn't blame or quarrel
With those who love, since Love directs
All those who love, of either sex,
Saddles their will, becomes their owner,
Then turns their burdens into honor!
Since he who had most knowledge bore
His burden, we should study more
And more for wisdom's sake the less

We know of love's unhappiness.
540   Love pays interest ten times over
      For every hardship that the lover
      Suffers on account of love,
      And that's the truth, as God's above.
      Love conquers all things, and until
      The end of time, love always will.

XVI *Berangier of the Long Ass*

GUERIN

The *Siddhi-kur*, a Mogul collection of tales, contains a story similar to *Berangier*, based evidently on a Sanskrit tale. Felix Liebrecht and Theodor Benfey believed that the Mogul story was the ancestor of our fabliau. Bédier (B 151–52, 449) convincingly argued against the Sanskrit tale as the ultimate source of the French tale since they have in common only their basic narrative traits.

Roy Pearcy offers a source of the two versions of our tale (*A*, anonymous, and *D*, our fabliau by Guerin) in Dagenet of Carlion, a character from the thirteenth-century prose romance *Lestoire de Merlin* who hacks up his own shield to impress his fellow knights with deeds he has not done. Pearcy claims that some narrative *X*, which descends from the Merlin episode, but which adds the fabliau motif of marital conflict, is the common source for both Guerin's fabliau and the anonymous version (*Romance Notes*, 1972).

Whether Pearcy's *X* existed or not, the marital conflict is the soul of Guerin's tale, providing the motivation and the rush toward the comic climax as the lady responds with energy and intelligence to her husband's ridiculous Falstaffian boasts. She earns Guerin's respect: "She was no common girl or fool."

> For two years I've been telling so
> Many fine tales and fabliaux
> Which I've discovered or made up
> That by St. John, it's time to stop
> And tell no more except this last,
> Called *Berangier of the Long Ass*,
> A story which you haven't heard,
> But if you'd like you'll hear it word
> For word this minute, no delay.
> 10 Hear it good people! Guerin will say
> What happened once in Lombardy,
> Where men aren't known for bravery,
> To a knight errant who'd been wed
> To a fine lady, purely bred
> And daughter to a landed earl.
> The young knight's father was a churl

Who'd gotten rich by usury.
His cellars were full; his grainery
Held all it could. He had cows and goats,
20   Dollars, deniers, marks, sous, and groats.
And the earl was deeply in his debt
With nothing left to pay, except
To give the rich man's son his daughter.
That's how good blood thins down to water,
How counts and earls and all their race
Decline and finish in disgrace.
If people wed to get out of debt,
Disgrace is what they ought to get.
The harm they do cannot be told:
30   From those who covet silver and gold
More than nobility, a race
Of foolish, good-for-nothing, base
And chickenhearted knights descends.
Thus chivalry declines and ends.
But here's the gist of what I heard
From start to finish as it occurred.
Not wasting any time, the earl
Put wedding garments on the girl
And married her to the young peasant,
40   Then dubbed him knight for a wedding present.
The young man went home with the maid.
For more than ten years, there they stayed.
This new knight valued relaxation,
Not valiant deeds or reputation:
The code of chivalry could go hang.
He loved pie, custard, and meringue,
But the common people he despised.
Now when the lady realized
How utterly her husband lacked
50   Virtue, how he was in fact
Useless for tournaments or war
And liked to fill a straw bed more
Than wield a lance or grasp a shield
(From which it clearly was revealed
To her that though the man was quite
A talker, he was not a knight
Worth talking of, but born and raised
A commoner), that's when she praised
The line of knights from whence she'd sprung,
60   Proud, valiant knights who'd never hung
Around the house from dawn to dark.

The husband knew that these remarks
Were aimed at him to put him down.
"Lady," he said, "I have renown.
I have more prowess than a dozen
Of your grandfathers. There's not a cousin
Or knight of any clan or class
Whose valor I do not surpass.
And I'm not lazy, take it from me.
70   Tomorrow morning you will see.
If I can find my foes tomorrow,
Who envy me and want to borrow
Trouble from me, I'll prove myself.
Not one will get off with his health.
These enemies who scorn and scoff
Will not scoff long with their heads off.
At dusk tomorrow they'll be dead."
For the time being, that's all he said.
        The knight arose at dawn next day
80   And rang a bell for his valet,
Who brought his buckler, sword, and lance
And armed his lord with elegance.
(The arms and armor all were splendid,
Not being dirtied, scratched, or dented.)
When he was geared and rigged for battle
And sitting proudly in the saddle,
He wondered what he should do next
To give his wife a good pretext
For thinking him a noble knight.
90   He saw a forest to his right
A quarter mile from his front door.
Without delay he headed for
The forest at a gallop. There
He had to gasp a bit for air.
He rode on further through the wood
To where a giant oak tree stood
And cast its shade upon a field.
He tied his horse, unhooked his shield,
And hung it from the lowest bough.
100   Listen to what the fool did now.
He drew his sword, shiny and bright,
And beat the shield with all his might,
Battering like a maniac,
Making it clatter at every whack,
Till he had mutilated it.
He took his sturdy lance and hit

The branch. The lance splintered in thirds.
His work was finished, so he spurred
His horse around the woods some more
110 Before arriving home. He bore
A third of his lance and but a fourth
Of the shield that he had carried forth.
He reined his horse. His wife came out
To ask what this was all about
And hold his stirrup strap in place,
But the knight hit her in the face
With the full weight of his big foot.
"Stand back!" he cried, "Hands off the boot!
Let it be known it isn't right
120 For you to touch so great a knight
As I am—not with my renown;
No such knight from Adam down
Adorns the family tree you've vaunted.
I'm not defeated, weak, or daunted.
I am the flower of chivalry!"
     The lady didn't disagree.
In consternation she beheld
The shattered lance and broken shield,
Not knowing what to think or say
130 About the evidence on display,
Afraid he'd beat her to the ground,
Because he threatened her and frowned.
She dared not touch, but stood somewhat
Out of his reach. Her mouth stayed shut.
What shall I say? He used this game
To vilify her family name
And put her in her place, that is,
To set her value under his.
     Another time the knight came back
140 With another shield all hewed and hacked
And full of holes. His chain-mail shirt,
However, was by no means hurt.
Neither was he—from head to foot
He wasn't bruised, he wasn't cut,
He wasn't even tired out.
That's when his wife began to doubt
Her husband's claim that he'd unhorsed,
Defeated, subjugated, forced
To pay homage, put to flight
150 And hanged two dozen enemy knights
That day. She saw that he concealed

His cowardice with a cracked shield,
And told herself if he went back
Into the woods again, she'd track
Him down to learn what foes he sought
And what he did and how he fought.
These were the plans she settled on.
  Early next day at break of dawn
Her husband armed and said he still
160 Had three more enemies to kill
Who kept on threatening and defying,
Causing disturbances and spying—
Crimes which the noble knight detested.
The lady tactfully suggested
He take some servants, three or four,
To make the victory more sure.
"Lady," he said, "I'll go alone.
I'll kill them so well on my own
Not one will get away with his life."
170 Urging his charger past his wife,
He sallied forth with zeal and zest
Into the woods. She rose and dressed
Herself in armor like a knight,
Mounted a stallion, held on tight,
Did not delay, did not look back
And followed in her husband's track
Till there he was in the same field
And from the same oak tree his shield
Was hanging. He was beating it,
180 Banging and making it submit
To a cruel martyrdom and rigor.
A person standing near might figure
A hundred devils were there yelling.
This isn't any joke I'm telling:
He raised a ruckus to the sky.
The lady reined her horse nearby.
At first the sight of this display
Of folly filled her with dismay.
But when she'd heard her fill of noise,
190 She shouted with a mighty voice
And urged her charger straight ahead:
"Sir Knight! Sir Knight! What folly led
You to come cutting up my manor?
Vain are my knighthood and my honor
If I don't slay you on this field.
Why are you picking on that shield?

What has it ever done to you?
You've bit off more than you can chew.
Fie on whoever says it's fit
200   For you to wage a war on it!"
And when he heard the speech she made,
He was dumbfounded and dismayed.
(His wife he didn't recognize.)
At once, great tears fell from his eyes
And his damasked sword fell from his grasp.
"Sir, for God's sake," he managed to gasp,
"Pity! If I've done any wrong,
I'll make it up. It won't take long.
I'll give whatever you want: my pony,
210   Lance—here's my shield, saddle, money."
The lady said, "As God's my shield,
Before you've parted from this field,
You'll change your tune. Now stop this noise.
I'm giving you an even choice.
Either you joust with me right now
(If so, you have my solemn vow
If you're unhorsed, you will not fail
To lose your head—it won't avail
To beg for pity or remorse),
220   Or let me get down from my horse
And I'll bend over on the grass
And you can come and kiss my ass
Right in the middle, if you please.
Just take whichever one of these
That suits your inclination. Choose!"
He who was shaking in his shoes,
Whose cowardliness no shame could oust,
Declared his purpose not to joust.
"Good Sir," he said, "I've deeply sworn
230   An oath to joust with no man born.
But be so kind as to dismount
And I'll do what it is your want."
The lady didn't wait around,
But lightly leapt upon the ground,
Stood with her back before his nose,
Lifted her tunic, touched her toes,
And said, "Your face goes here, Sir Knight."
But when her crevice came in sight,
It seemed to him the ass and cunt
240   Were one long crack from back to front.
He thought it surely must have been

The longest ass he'd ever seen.
And there he placed the kiss of truce,
Which cowards customarily use,
Next to the hole. That's how she served
The knight what richly he deserved.
The lady stood, turned round and mounted.
Before she left, her husband shouted,
"Tell me your name, sir, since you're leaving.
250 Then go in peace. We'll call it even."
—"Vassal, I'll tell it. I don't mind.
Another such name you will not find:
All other men are beneath my class.
I'm Berangier of the Long Ass,
Who puts to shame the chickenhearted."
     The wife had finished what she'd started.
Now she returned home through the wood,
Disarmed herself as best she could
And sent for the knight she held above
260 All others in esteem and love.
She led him into the bed chamber,
Where with an eager kiss he claimed her.
And when the husband reached the house,
She, who did not fear her spouse,
Didn't even deign to stir,
But made her lover sit by her.
And when the knight came in the room,
Afflicted by despair and gloom,
The sight of a lover with his wife
270 Was not the high point of his life.
"Madam," he said, "it's plain to me
That you have done me injury,
Bringing a man to my abode.
You'll pay for this my girl. You've sowed
And you shall reap." —"Shut up, you bore!"
She said, "And don't say anymore,
Because one more insinuation
Against my name and reputation
And by the saints I'll file a claim
280 Against you for my injured fame.
Go on, you cuckold! Go on, be jealous!"
—"You'll file a claim? And who, pray tell us,
Will hear a claim that comes from you?"
—"Your fellow knight at arms is who,
Who subjugated you today,
I mean my lord Sir Berangier

Of the Long Ass, who will disgrace
You once again!" The husband's face
Turned fiery red with rage and shame.
290   No more could he abuse her name.
He felt checkmated. He felt ill.
And from that day, she did her will:
She was no common girl or fool.
When the shepherd's weak, the wolf shits wool.

XVII   *Aloul*

This fabliau could be subtitled "The Busy Night." It presents four sexual encounters and no less than nine physical or verbal encounters in a tale which
can be divided into six linear episodes: the garden, the bedroom, the lean-to,
back to the bedroom, the top of the stairs, and the storeroom. Each episode is
triggered by the preceding one, except when the priest returns to the bedroom,
which can be explained by his desire not to leave any business unfinished.

It is a typical fabliau, pitting a "lewd" priest, a beautiful lady, and her ugly,
vilain husband. Yet the author garnishes it with passages of entertaining parody:
parody of courtly literature (ll. 41–60, the garden scene), and of epic literature
(ll. 604 ff., the various single or mass fighting scenes). These are not sustained
parodies, for the tale remains, as a whole, unmistakably a fabliau. The crude
line (l. 63) interrupting the courtly description of the *hortus*, clearly indicates the
tone which the tale is going to take.[1] As in *The Wife of Orleans*, the husband
will be cuckolded and beaten, but he will certainly not be content.

The long fabliau (987 lines in the original) leaves one almost exhausted but,
as Muscatine points out, somewhat disappointed at its trivial ending (M 49).

> Whoever wants to hear the full
> Authentic story of Aloul
> Will hear enough if he won't fail
> To listen to each good detail.
> Aloul was wealthier than Caesar,
> But Lord! he was a stingy geezer.
> He never thought he had enough.
> Money was his chiefest love
> And point and purpose of his life.
> He had a lovely, noble wife.
> A year before on their wedding day,
> A lord had given her away
> For cash, which there was plenty of.
> The writings tell us Aloul's love
> Grew so intense, that wake or sleeping,
> He could not trust her out of his keeping.

10

---

[1] Hortus = garden or orchard. A typical love setting in courtly literature.

This jealousy was a bad deal
For Aloul, since he couldn't feel
Insured from misery. Aloul
20   Proved himself a perfect fool
When such a business he took on.
(He *will* be busy, dawn to dawn,
Trying to watch her every move.)
Here's the kind of fool he proved:
She couldn't go to church without
An escort always hanging about.
Guess who the escort was? Aloul!—
Always suspicious she might fool
Him with a secret assignation.
30   The lady saw with indignation
How matters went from bad to worse
And swore unless she took the first
Opportunity she had
To fool her husband, she was mad.
She couldn't sleep or rest at all.
Her husband's loving made her ill.
What could she do, how wreak some cruel
And fitting vengeance on Aloul
For blaming her without foundation?
40   She got no sleep or relaxation.
      Thus her bitterness dragged on
Until one lovely April dawn
Sweet scents and birdsong filled the air
And love seemed blooming everywhere.
The nightingale upon the bough
Sang so sweet and clearly now
That everything for love was dying.
The lady, after hours of lying
Awake, by indignation tortured,
50   Got up and stepped into the orchard
Barefoot on the dewy lawn.
She had a long gray mantle on
And on her neck a shawl of fur.
And now the parson noticed her.
She was up early; so was he.
He lived in their vicinity—
Between their lands were just some trees.
There was a pleasant morning breeze.
The sun was rising in the east.
60   The air was warm. Here came the priest,
Saw her and was deeply charmed:

How perfectly she had been formed!
How dearly he would like to tup her!
He'd bet his tunic and his supper
That he would have his way with her.
The priest stepped forward, calm and sure,
Wise, self-possessed and undismayed.
"Lady, good day to you," he said.
"Why up so early? Tell me true."
70   —"Sir," she answered him, "the dew
Is healthful on an April morning,
Refreshing, bracing and restoring—
At least the doctors tell me so."
—"Lady, I agree. You know,
Getting up at dawn is good,
But one should breakfast on a food
Whose parts I have investigated.
It's over there, where I can't get it.
The root of it is short and thick,
80   But for a woman, well or sick,
It's very healthful medicine."
—"Don't waste time. Climb over then,"
The lady answered, "if you please,
And kindly show me where it is."
—"I'll be right there!" the priest exclaimed,
Not wasting time. Over he came
And stood beside the lady now:
"Madam, you must sit down. That's how
This beneficial herb is plucked."
90   And she agreed, not being struck
By any metaphoric meaning.
(Pray God Aloul, in bed and dreaming,
Doesn't learn what's going on.)
There on the grass, his wife sat down.
The priest, who at this song and dance
Was well-accomplished, dropped his pants,
Flopped the lady down, and then
Demonstrated the medicine.
She shoved and slithered out from under.
100   "Get up!" she cried, "What have you done, sir?
Get out! What shall I do? You men!
I'll never trust a priest again!"
The parson jumped up to his feet.
(His satisfaction was complete.)
"Lady, there's nothing left to do.
I am your lover, loyal, true.

I'll do your every wish and want!"
"Sir," she said, "this incident—
Please keep it quiet, please don't say
110   A word of it, and I will pay.
All your life, you'll be well off.
But as for me, I've had it rough
For two long years as Aloul's wife
And not a moment's joy. His life
Is hateful to me. He's a cruel
And jealous brute. A man's a fool
Who guards his wife, humiliates,
Watches, spies and calculates.
But by the Child that Mary suckled,
120   I'm going to change his name to Cuckold!
From now on, you and I are friends.
This very night, when the moon descends,
Come to me—no hesitating.
I'll be ready, sir, and waiting
To give you comfort and release."
"Your mercy, Lady," said the priest.
"Deserves my thanks. Thank you. I fear
We should be getting out of here.
Your lord, Aloul, may be here soon.
130   You think on me, and I on you."
They said goodbye and did not stay.
Each left and went a separate way.
Back to the house the lady sped.
Her lord was fuming in his bed.
"Lady, where've you been?" he cried.
—"My lord," she answered him, "outside.
Out in the orchard near the kitchen."
—"What? Outside? Without permission?
Little respect you show your master."
140   The lady didn't even answer.
What use in talking anymore?
Her husband cursed at her and swore
That if she let this scene repeat
Itself, he'd shame her in the street.
He said no more, but leapt upright,
Worried, spoiling for a fight,
Suspicious he'd been made a cuckold.
Jealousy kept him bound and buckled
And led him anywhere it pleased.
150   Around about, both west and east
He searched the farm, seeking a clue

Of some forbidden rendez vous,
Till in an orchard path he stood.
The morning air was sweet and good.
He searched and sniffed until he found
The dew rubbed off along the ground
Here and there about the orchard.
By anger and suspicion tortured,
Onward through the trees he snooped.
160   All of a sudden, his foot slipped
Right where his wife slipped earlier
When the priest tumbled on top of her.
He searched some more until he found
Heel prints planted in the ground
And toe tracks printed in between.
By now Aloul was seeing green
Because he knew—he had the proof!
The place itself proclaimed the truth—
That someone else had plowed his field.
170   How must his findings be revealed?
If there was stronger proof to get,
He didn't want a scandal yet,
Before her guilt was clear as dawn.
(She was in danger from now on
Unless she watched each move she made.)
       The afternoon began to fade.
Aloul returned now to his dwelling,
Careful to keep his face from telling
His wife the trouble he was brewing.
180   Supper on the stove was stewing.
The serving folk sat down and ate.
The beds were made. Since it was late,
The cowherds all got bedded down.
Aloul had on his sleeping gown.
He and his wife stood by the bed.
"Lady," he said, "you go ahead
And get in first, beside the wall,
Since I'll be getting up to call
The cowherds soon, to get them going,
190   Wake them up and get them plowing
Out in the field to earn their keep."
—"Sir, you go first," she said. "I'll sleep
On this side, thank you. I don't lie
At ease beside the wall. My thigh
Is sore. A nail beneath the straw
Over there has rubbed it raw.

Next to the wall I'm not at ease."
At last, in order to appease
His wife, he went to bed before her
200   And didn't double-check the door or
See that the bolt had not been pulled.
Aloul had been beguiled and gulled;
Soon he was snoring, sound asleep.
    Now came the parson, step by step
And found the outside door unbarred.
He nudged it quietly ajar,
Opened it just a couple of inches,
And then he peed upon the hinges.
Inside there was a howling bitch.
210   The priest, however, didn't flinch
Or move a limb; he kept on peeing
Because he didn't care a bean
For the bitch's bark. But when she smelled
And heard the priest, she hurled herself
In fury on him, seized his gown,
And if he hadn't turned around
And reached the bedroom doorway fast,
The pause he took would have been his last.
Without a sound, the door swung wide,
220   Then shut. The priest was safe inside,
The bitch locked out, the hateful hound!
He loathed the way she snarled and howled.
She was a menace to his calling—
Always eating, biting, mauling,
And now he's safe behind the door.
But midnight's struck! It's late! That cur
Delayed him more than he had reckoned.
    Meanwhile, Aloul had been awakened
After a painful, long and drawn-
230   Out dream that he had undergone.
It left him panic-stricken, weeping.
It seemed somehow, as he lay sleeping,
That suddenly that night there came in
A priest, all tonsured, crowned and shaven,
Who seized his wife and stretched her flat
Underneath him on the mat
And tasted of his lady's favors
While Aloul couldn't move to save her.
No, there was nothing he could do,
240   Until a cow began to moo
And startled him from dream's dissembling.

Now he was awake and trembling,
Fearing his wife might come to harm.
He kissed and clutched her with his arm,
And then he grabbed her by the breast.
(She wasn't getting any rest.
She had to be awake and wary.)
As for the priest, he didn't tarry.
Step by step he made his way
250   To where the wife and husband lay,
While she lay listening in fright.
"How bad I feel! I can't sleep right.
Take your hand away," she said;
"Get back! You're hogging all the bed.
Why, I can hardly move my knees!"
—"These women! God, they're hard to please!"
Aloul retreated in a huff.
The priest climbed on as he got off
And perked the wife up, head to heel.
260   Aloul turned over and could feel
The bed atremble—*creek* and *crack*—
As if somebody rode horseback
On it. His wife! What was the matter?
She didn't usually make this clatter.
Beneath the cover Aloul reached
And felt, between her arms, the priest!
He kept on probing all about
Up and down and in and out.
He wanted to scream out loud, but didn't.
270   And then he grasped the priest's equipment,
Grabbed and yanked and cried and yelped:
"Arise! Arise, my people! Help!
Son of a bitch! Get up with you!
Somebody's come—I don't know who—
Made me a cuckold in my bed!"
The lady jumped upon his head
And grabbed him by the adam's apple.
The priest was trying to ungrapple
The husband's fingers from his balls.
280   He jerked away so hard, he sprawled
All the way to the fire place.
(He'd had his lesson now. His face
And flesh were bruised. He'd had it rough.
But what did he care? All for love,
He'd gladly suffer grief and pain.)
Aloul's cowherds were up again.

One took a club, another a stick.
The priest, unless he made a quick
Departure would be beat and shamed
290   Because the crowd was so inflamed
By Aloul's cries and imprecations.
Commotion reigned, and agitation.
From everywhere the people raced.
The priest could find no hiding place
Except a lean-to, where the sheep
And lambs lay down at night to sleep.
He hid there quiet, still as dead.
    Great was the uproar in the bed,
Where Aloul and the lady fought.
300   The husband was so overwrought
He gasped for breath and started coughing.
His servants pulled the lady off him.
But he wouldn't quit. Again he called
His cowherds to resume the brawl.
Once again began the rout.
He sought and searched with his sword out
Back and forth and down and up.
There wasn't a kettle or a tub
Or pot the cowherds left unturned,
310   And thus they knew, that's how they learned
Aloul was dreaming: all this fuss
Over a thing that never was!
"Let it alone, my lord," they said;
You need some sleep. Go back to bed.
This was some fancy in the night."
—"Go to the valleys! Search the heights!"
Cried he who would not be sidetracked:
"When these two hands have got him trapped,
What will you have to say then, eh?
320   What? Shall I let him get away?
Look for him in the shop—the loft!
Look upstairs, downstairs, in the trough
And underneath the step. Whoever
Finds him first has done a favor
For me, when he has brought him here.
He'll get two pecks of wheat this year
On Christmas day, and wages too."
The cowherds, when they heard this new
Incentive, coveted the grain.
330   Here and there they went again,
Hunting, searching, left and right.

(Unless he's hidden snug and tight,
This priest will lose his family jewels.)
A woman servant of Aloul's,
Hortense by name, who lived with them,
Old and fat and full of phlegm,
Straight to where the priest was lurking
Came through the lean-to, looking, searching,
Without a lamp to pierce the black.

340 She woke the sheep and shooed them back
And kept on groping, feeling, prying
Nearer to where the priest was hiding.
The priest still had his trousers down.
His balls were swollen, big and round.
Down they hung like sacks of wool.
The hair around was thick and full
As I-don't-know-what trick of speech.
As chance would have it, Hortense reached
A pair of balls she thought belonged

350 To a large sheep, but she was wrong.
She raised her hand a bit and found
It hairy there and very round,
With a small valley in the middle.
Uncertain how to treat this riddle,
The woman hastily pulled back.
It was the priest, who was awake.
He grappled Hortense by the loins,
Pulled her to him till they joined
So tight his balls hung from her crotch.

360 Hortense was flabbergasted. Ouch!
What should she do? If she should shout,
Scores of men would come pouring out
And witness what was happening.
Better not to say a thing
Or utter even a syllable.
So Hortense, whether she will or nil,
Bore what the priest was doing with her
Without a cry, a word, a whisper.
What choice had she? She'd no defense!

370 "I am the priest," he said, "Hortense.
I visited your lady's bed
Tonight, but was perceived, and fled.
And now I stand in deadly peril.
I need some help from you, old girl.
If you can get me out of here,
I'll love you tenderly, I swear

By all my books and manuscripts!"
The woman puckered up her lips,
But said, "Fear not, sir, have no doubt.
380   I'll do my best to get you out,"
Then backed away and left him, running.
Hortense was full of wiles and cunning.
With indignation in her voice,
She cried aloud, "Hey there, you boys,
You oxherds, bastards, dunderheads!
What are you after? Back to your beds!
Back to your filthy straw! Lie down!
To think of how my lady's thrown
Her kindly deeds away on you!
390   And now I see the saying's true:
A churl will hate like steaming hell
Anyone who treats him well—
That's how a churl shows gratitude!
My lady cares for nothing lewd.
She is a lady, good and pure.
Her reputation is secure—
And you won't even let her be!
I swear to God, if I were she,
You'd get no handouts—cheese or bacon—
400   You'd have to give back what you've taken.
Peas and bread would be your diet.
Whoever named you *churls* was right.
Churl comes from *churlish*. That's a fact.
What are you hunting, fools? Get back!
Why are you making this commotion?"
When they had heard her exhortation
And understood Hortense's threat,
The cowherds feared they wouldn't get
The bacon that their bellies needed.
410   All together then they pleaded
Their self-defense and made excuses:
"Our master did it! Don't accuse us.
He gives the word, we just obey.
But this we promise: from this day
We're going to leave our lady be.
She gives to us ungrudgingly.
She is a wise and prudent dame.
The way he treats her is a shame.
He shouldn't be suspicious of her.
420   But they've made peace now. He's discovered
He was mistaken. He'll sleep instead

Of quarreling." They also went to bed.
   But Aloul had to scold and school
His lady not to make a fool
Of him for everyone to see.
"God," she murmured, "lucky me,
With such a lord, whose lifelong aim
Is to protect my flesh from shame.
Curse such marriages as his!

430   And curse the kin whose fault it is
For giving me to such a man.
Morning, noon and night I can
Not find a moment's rest or ease.
He seeks and seeks but never sees
Anything to blame me for.
He'll have a tiresome, tedious chore
Trying to catch me in the wrong.
He'll have to watch me close and long,
Waiting for me to make a slip."

440   —"Lady," he answered, "go to sleep
And leave me alone now, damn your hide."
Aloul rolled over on his side
And made believe that he was sleeping.
   When all was still, the priest came creeping
Out of the shed, still hot and bothered,
Straight to the couple's bed, and slithered
Between the sheets beside his lover.
Aloul, awake beneath the cover,
Rocked with the rolling of their haunches

450   And all too painfully was conscious
They were united as a pair.
Two against one—that wasn't fair!
Their two against his one might be
Able to do him injury.
Attack might turn into a rout.
He softly pulled his saber out,
Stealthily got out of bed,
And stormed out to the cowherds' shed:
"What? Sleeping, Robert? Hey! Sit up!

460   I swear to God, whoever tupped
My wife is back and doing more
And eviler things than he did before
To me with her. Arise! Attack!
Wake up your men! Let's pay him back!
If you can catch this foe of ours,
Valuable prizes will be yours—

A hat for each, or coat, or both!"
Then all the cowherds swore an oath
On hearing all this promising,
470   A badass mass this priest would sing
If once their fists could reach his hide.
While they were speaking, just outside
The house and leaning up against
The cowherds' doorway, stood Hortense,
Hearing everything they said,
The plans and projects that they made
(Which all would turn to Aloul's shame).
Quickly to the priest she came:
"Get up, my lord," she cried, "be gone."
480   The priest would have been moving on,
But dressed too slowly. He'd regret
That soon enough, because he met
Aloul, who came as he was leaving.
"Oops," said the priest, "Hi there, good evening."
The husband leapt into the air,
Came down and grabbed the priest's thick hair:
"Son of a bitch, I've got you now.
Help! Lend a hand," he shouted, "Ow!
Don't let him get away! Hold on!"
490   You should have seen the cowherds run
To help him out. One pushed, one shoved,
All struck like fools at blind man's bluff.
They took Aloul to be the priest,
Battered his back and bones and pressed
And pinned and held him to the ground.
The priest, meanwhile, with one great bound
Escaped, but where? He wasn't sure.
It was too dark. Where was the door?
All he wanted now was out.
500   But then he came upon a stout
And heavy threshing pole and found
A winnowing basket, strong and sound,
For winnowing the wheat that year.
He found them leaning by a stair,
Grabbed them, climbed the stairway, made
A sturdy wicker barricade,
And took his stand there, battle-ready.
They'd have to name the priest's goddaddy
To reach the priest and not get crowned.
510   As long as he could stand his ground,
He was secure within his hold.

Meanwhile Aloul, whose men had rolled
And trampled him, was still in trouble.
What kept the blows from being double
Was that they knew him when he cursed.
No bear could have been beaten worse,
Caught in a peasant's trap, than he,
If he hadn't cried, "You're beating *me*!"
Now when they recognized their lord,
520   They couldn't figure out a word
To say, but stood there, sore and sad.
"Sir," they asked, "are you hurt bad?"
—"Naw. I've had worse. To hell with it.
Go on and get a fire lit
And do what you swore you'd do tonight."
    After they got the fire bright,
Throughout the house the cowherds hunted.
Robert, the most ambitious, wanted
To do his master's will the best.
530   He started up the stairs the priest
Would be defending from above.
But Robert couldn't see enough
To get prepared for being blasted.
He pushed and poked the winnowing basket
And shoved it roughly to the left.
The priest stepped forward, staff aloft,
And gave Bob's backbone such a crack
It sent him catapulting back
Down to the middle of the floor.
540   (He'd got what he was asking for.
If Robert felt unfairly served,
I'd say he got what he deserved—
Why did he go and look for trouble?)
    Here came Aloul with all his rabble.
"Hey, are you hurt? What happened, Robert?"
—"Yes, sir," he answered. "I've been clobbered.
My bones have all been numbered twice.
Sir, I don't know what Antichrist
Struck me backward on the stair.
550   My heart's in need of some repair.
I think I'm going back to bed."
The cowherds swarmed the stair and said,
"What's hiding up there?" Then they raised
Their torches high, and by the blaze
They looked—and lo, the priest was there,
Lurking on the upper stair,

Leaning over on his shield.
And when they saw the staff he wielded,
One and all, they crowded back,
560   Fearing that he might attack.
Aloul, however, drew his sword.
Valiantly advancing toward
The priest, with righteous wrath inflamed,
Onward, up the steps he came.
Four steps he climbed (or three at least),
Then listened—nothing from the priest.
At last Aloul called out, "Who's there?"
—"I am the priest! Get off my stair!
You toy of fortune, fool of fate,
570   What is this, Lent? Is it that late?
I thought it wasn't yet Noel.
This stick will bend your sinful skull.
Whoever here experiences
My stick is sure to lose his senses."
Between the cowherds and the pastor,
Loud outcries rose. Aloul climbed faster.
At last he reached the winnowing basket,
Stood before it, swung and bashed it
With his keenly cutting steel.
580   The priest, his enemy, could feel
His fort and citadel attacked.
He heaved his threshing weapon back
And hit Aloul so hard and gave
Him such a spin, Aloul could save
No time for snacks as he came down.
Sad and befuddled on the ground,
Aloul had nothing left to say.
"Aloul, Aloul!" the priest called, "Hey!
This stick of mine has wasps that sting,
590   And they resent your trespassing.
You cowherds, test your welcome! Pluck
Your courage up and try your luck.
You might gain entry to my halls,
But if you break your valuables
Trying, don't come to me to mend them.
My walls are strong, and I defend them.
These ramparts aren't a cinch to scale!"
        You should have heard the cowherds rail
And curse by Earth and Sea and Sun.
600   But long before the priest had done,
They'd be so tuckered and exhausted,

Hot and strained and worn and wasted,
They could have been skinned and not have cared.
   Once again, the great war flared
Between the cowherds and the priest.
Bitter and long would be the siege.
Around the steps and in formation,
The cowherds shouted indignation.
For Aloul's fall they all expected
610 Revenge, and quickly they erected
Beanpoles, ladders, scaffolds, chairs
And benches all about the stairs
To make a way to reach the priest,
Who held his own, and like a beast
At bay so savagely fought back
That anyone who launched attack,
Armored and armed however well,
Fierce, valorous or hardy, fell
Backwards, beaten down the stair,
620 Because the priest was well aware
That if they got their hands on him
The chances would be very slim
His honor would be left intact.
   The cowherd Steven now attacked,
One of the toughest, mean and strong,
His stick so heavy, thick and long
That he could hardly get it up.
Out of a thousand, who could hope
To find a better man than Steven?
630 He was bolder than Robert even,
More aggressive, brave and forward.
He would have thought himself a coward
Not to avenge his lord's defeat.
He was the one who always beat
The drum at Sunday caroling.
Steven didn't say a thing;
Up he stepped and with his stick
Gave the parson such a lick
He backed him up against the stair
640 And then closed in and by the hair
Grappled the priest and bent him double.
Fearing his flesh would be uncoupled,
The parson gnashed his teeth and reared,
Then caught the cowherd's neck and beard
And squeezed him till his knuckles cracked,
And Steven angrily squeezed back.

They locked so tight, a single mare
Might have carried them a year,
Galloping, without their falling.
650   Now all the cowherds started calling:
"Arise! Let's storm the steps my lord,
With sticks and clubs! You take your sword.
Let's go and give our comrade aid."
When all their forces were arrayed,
They charged upstairs in one formation.
And when he saw retaliation
Imminent upon the steps,
The priest strove hard and bit his lips
And yanked his foe so hard he flopped
660   Him upside under him and toppled
Him down the steps against his will,
Eyes apopping as he fell,
Bones a-cracking. All the rest
Found themselves in sore distress,
Couldn't find a firm foothold
And couldn't keep from being bowled
Down the steps that they'd misstepped.
The man that they assaulted swept
The cowherds down the whole long flight.
670   (They had attained to such a height
Their brains failed, their wits were jumbled.)
Necks upon the stairway tumbled.
Head and hips and ribs and feet
And butts upon the stairway beat.
They counted steps more accurately
Descending, backbone over knee,
Than when they had been climbing higher.
And now they rolled into the fire,
Hot, intense and burning cruelly.
680   The pain and punishment were gruelling
Beneath the pile. "My feet!" one cried;
"My head!" another cried. "My hide!"
"My back!" "Oh, God, my burning chest!"
        And now I'll tell you how the priest
Came to grief and his luck failed.
Clearing the landing, he was nailed
By Berengier the strong and stout.
He was one cowherd! He was a lout!
He herded the mares. Yes, that was he.
690   The likes of him you'll never see.
One eye straight and the other eye crooked,

Cross-eyed sideways is how he looked,
One foot right and the other foot wrong.
He held the priest with a hold so strong
On one of his feet that he wouldn't let
The priest go where he wanted to get.
Stout Berengier let out a yell:
"You worthless people! What the hell
Are you doing? Help me! Hurry up!
700   Everybody come and help
Castrate this priest! If he escapes
So help me God, we've lost the capes
Our master promised—and the hats!"
    Believe you me, when the priest heard that,
He wasn't altogether thrilled.
He twisted his leg and jerked and pulled
So frantically he freed his foot,
Though Berengier still held the boot
And jacket hostage. He didn't mind.
710   Better pawn them than leave behind
His other business. He believed
That it was time for him to leave.
Here there was nothing left to do.
Immediately the cowherds, too,
Tumbled out of the house, behind him,
With sticks and clubs. They thought they'd find him
Inside the barn—and he *was* there,
His knees tucked up, up in the air
Hanging stilly from a rafter.
720   They all came tramping, stamping after
Into the barn, looked left and right,
And saw no one, no priest in sight.
They wondered, could they be spellbound?
Even the wisest of them found
Nothing to say. They stood there stunned.
What strange enchantment had he spun,
This priest, around them now? Sore, mad,
Huffy and feeling they'd been had,
Out of the barn the cowherds poured
730   And hurried to inform their lord
Of what had happened, that is to say,
The priest had gotten clean away.
"What, got away? Damn!" said Aloul.
"And I'm supposed to stay a fool
And cuckold now. Will no one free
Me from this priest? His life will be

My bane until I have revenge.
If you would like to be my friends,
Spy for me some more instead
740   Of giving up. I'm going to bed.
I'm wounded in the side and chest.
Curses be on such a guest.
I'll never know a moment's peace
Till I have vengeance on this priest
Who got me cut and cuckolded."
And now Aloul went back to bed,
Saying, "Boys, keeping looking round,
In the house and on the grounds.
He's got to be somewhere. I bet
750   He hasn't left my manor yet.
Therefore, if he is on my lands
Somewhere, he'll fall into our hands."
—"Yes, sir, that's right. I hope he does,"
The cowherds said. "But what about us?
Here we've been up and on our feet
And worked all night. We need to eat.
We're all exhausted to the bone."
—"Well then," replied Aloul, "go on.
Eat, but don't be sleeping mind you!
760   The darkest part of night's behind you.
Soon seeing shouldn't be so tough."
    Now the cowherds all went off
And got a great big fire going.
Conversation started flowing.
They whispered while the fire hissed
About the exploits of the priest.
When they had whispered all they wanted,
Told and retold and recounted,
Their talk returned to food and drink.
770   (That's the way that cowherds think.
They're never glad unless they're eating.)
Robert, who held the mace for meting
The orders out, sent someone after
A slab of bacon from a rafter
Up in the barn— "and make damn sure
You get a big, fat side, well-cured,
So all can have enough to eat."
Berengier got to his feet,
Obedient to the command,
780   And went on out, his knife in hand,
A sharp steel dagger, finely tempered.

He trudged across the yard and entered
Into the barn and came below
The bacons hanging in a row.
Along the row he poked and pried,
Looking for the fattest side.
(That was his customary test:
The fattest slabs are always best.)
Along he felt, from cut to cut,
790 Until he caught the parson's butt,
Found some soft and hard spots in it,
And figured out it must be rennet,
Since that's how rennet's usually stored.
Up and back his hands explored
Until he reached the parson's knees.
"Let's see now," he concluded; "these
Are beef arms hanging till they've dried."
But Berengier was mystified
That here were such accoutrements.
800 Downward now his fingers went
And came upon the parson's tool.
Since it was soft, he couldn't tell
What it was that he was feeling,
Drying and hanging from the ceiling,
Sausage, maybe, tripes or what?
"Anyway," he said, "I'll cut
It off. This meat should make a meal."
The priest could hear and feel the steel
Across his genitalia stealing;
810 Then his departure from the ceiling
Was swift. He plummeted like stone,
Struck and crushed the cowherd's bones.
Berengier, battered, broken necked,
Thought, "What an idiot, to neglect
To bring along my tallow lamp."
Back to the fire the cowherd limped,
So crippled he could hardly stand:
"Help me, Sir Cowherds, lend a hand!"
Help me lift that bacon back.
820 When the rope broke, it fell and cracked
Me in the neck. It almost burst
My neck right here. It did! God curse
The butcher who didn't hang it right!"
You should have seen them run for light,
Light the house up like a beacon
And then go looking for the bacon

With Berengier, to try to tell
Why it was the bacon fell.
Inside the barn the cowherds found
830   No slab or side upon the ground.
None was where it shouldn't be.
They all were hanging—twenty-three—
Hanging in order from the rafter.
Then everyone spoke up in laughter.
Some shouted, "Berengier won't get
Close to the bacon even yet!"
And then another cowherd said,
"Berengier must have been afraid
The priest was lurking not far off."
840   —"Sirs!" said Berengier, "enough!
Now let the matter rest, will you?
But I speak well and I speak true:
A bacon where the hams are hanging
Fell down, I swear! I felt it banging
My neck! Besides, there was some rennet
That had some soft and hard spots in it.
Explain what *that* could be, at least!"
—"I think," they said, "it was the priest.
His legs are what you must have found,
850   Where he was hiding off the ground.
Look, maybe we'll find him after all."
Berengier looked back and saw
The priest behind the door, but didn't
Recognize him, for he was hidden
By night and darkness where he crouched.
Berengier reached out and touched.
The priest could feel and understand
Berengier's eye and now his hand
Were on him. Now he would be known!
860   Between the neck and collar bone
With his great clenched square fist he beat
And crumpled the cowherd at his feet.
"Go," he said, "Sir Berengier.
Are you contented with your pay?
Take up your bed and walk, my son.
Your sin is washed away and gone.
You've done sufficient penance, cowherd.
Now, have these friends of yours step forward
To join you in the benediction.
870   Fools will seek a fool's direction—
I couldn't call you clever yet,

Since you of all people couldn't get
A message straight without a stick.
These wasps are swarming, fast and thick.
They like to have their little fun,
So have your friends come forward, one
And all and join you in the blessing."
You should have seen the cowherds pressing
Upon the priest from every side.
880   He'll soon be disciplined, chastised,
Unless he fights with tooth and fist.
Robert Cowherd jumped up first.
His right hand clutched the priest's midriff.
The priest pulled back and with his left
Gave him such a backhand buffet
He almost died from the anguish of it.
He would have been manhandled more
If cowherds, cowherds by the score,
Distressed to see their friends distressed,
890   Hadn't swarmed the priest and pressed
And kept on crowding, fast and thick—
But not too close to the priest's stick.
(They'd learned about his stick before!)
Now there was such a great uproar,
Aloul awoke and up he sat.
What a commotion! What was that
Making a din like the world would end?
And then he thought—it was his friend
The priest, who'd broken in once more.
900   He leapt up, grabbed his sword and tore
Down to the barn and hurtled smack
Into the center of the pack
And seized the parson from behind.
The priest hauled back and knocked him blind
Right in the face, into the lap
Of one of the cowherds.
                     Now I'll wrap
This story up. No use in stalling:
From all sides, cowherds came assaulting
The priest. In vain was his defense.
910   They pinned him down. That's how it ends,
Because Aloul addressed his gang:
"Should he be killed, men? Or just hanged?"
And they replied of one accord,
"We need such vengeance that when word
Gets out we'll all be famous. This calls,

My lord, for cutting off his balls."
—"Cut?" he said, "I thought we'd drown . . .
You've got a point! I think you've found
An answer. I *will* take your advice.
920   Men, let's go ahead and slice!
So get a move on now. Don't wait—
Go get a razor. We'll castrate
This priest and then go back to bed."
    But when the priest heard what he said,
And understood, he was no fool.
Sweetly he addressed Aloul:
"Aloul, for Christian charity,
I beg you, don't disfigure me.
Aloul, have mercy on a sinner."
930   —"Priest, unconditional surrender
Is all you get. I give no quarter."
The priest could hardly hold his water.
From now on, he was stunned, dismayed.
They went and got the razor blade
And knocked the parson off his feet.
They had to rough him up and beat
Some more to turn him over. They flogged
Him upside down, then got a log
And jammed it up between his legs:
940   "And now who wants to crack his eggs?
Here's the razor. Who will it be?"
—"I will," said Berengier. "Let me!
I'll gladly cut the son of a bitch's
Balls off." Off came the parson's britches.
Berengier bent down and gripped
The portion that he meant to clip.
The priest's position was looking grimmer.
    But now the wife, with torch aglimmer,
Came swooping down upon Aloul
950   And all his men. She grabbed a stool
With three strong legs and a hard seat.
With all her strength and weight, she beat
Berengier in the backbone,
Knocked him down and stretched him prone.
He almost died. Then with a hook,
Hortense, who came behind her, struck
His ribs. The tallow lamp blew out.
Panic-stricken, in a rout,
The cowherds fled. The women flailed
960   And thrashed about till they unjailed

And threw the priest out. Then he fled
The premises. And well he did:
Into unfriendly hands he'd fallen.
Downhearted, battered, beat, crestfallen,
His hair all sticking up, blood-spattered,
His jacket hanging down in tatters,
His shirt in shreds, a pant leg gone,
One of his boots still left in pawn,
Out of danger, away he ran.
970   But he had suffered much, poor man.

XVIII   *Saint Peter and the Jongleur*

This fabliau, with a very well-made plot, draws laughter from its ironic situation: Saint Peter plays a crap game with the disreputable jongleur, who suspects the saint is cheating, and gambling becomes the path of redemption. The jongleur is portrayed as the typical happy-go-lucky, good-hearted jongleur and attracts our sympathy because of his extreme poverty and eternal bad luck (see the thieves in *Hearmie*).

D. D. R. Owen considers this fabliau a blasphemous parody of the Harrowing of Hell (JO 105). But the author does not present us the Hell of the theologians but rather a fanciful reenactment of the jongleur's hellish life: in Hell, he continues to gamble without suffering the expected torments. Even fire does not serve to torment but to warm him, as it did in the tavern (see Cooke, OF 198, 199).

> It shouldn't be astonishing
> When a good thought or a good thing
> Is expressed with eloquence.
> A certain jongleur lived in Sens
> In poverty and destitution.
> He never had a decent suit on.
> Whether the wind blew warm or colder,
> He walked with nothing on his shoulders
> Except his shirt. He was so poor
> 10   The only thing he ever wore
> To keep his feet warm was one used,
> Flipfloppy, mismatched pair of shoes,
> Which were so full of cracks and holes
> The light broke through top, sides, and soles.
> Often his fiddle was in pawn,
> His jacket lost, his tunic gone.
> His pants were what he mostly clung to.
> His shirt was just some rags that hung to
> His neck. He didn't dress to please
> 20   The eye. In taverns he took his ease—
> There and brothels—between the one

And the other, what a life of fun!
Taverns were where he passed the day.
Dicing and drinking took his pay.
Nothing pleased the jongleur more
Than dicing with a drunk or whore.
With his green cap on, the man always
Wished work days could be all feast days.
Sundays always came too slowly.
30   He hated fights and feuds. He wholly
Gave himself up to foolish, cheap sin.
Here's how he had to cash his chips in:
In foolish sinning he abused
His time, and when his time was used,
He died of various diseases.
A devil, one who never ceases
Laying snares for people, stole
Up to his body to snatch his soul.
Poor devil, for a month he'd been
40   Wandering the world and couldn't win
One soul. So when the jongleur passed,
This devil reached his bedside fast.
And since he died in sin, none came
Down to dispute the devil's claim;
And so the devil bore him down
To his hot hostel underground.
Swarms of imps from everywhere
Were bringing in the souls they'd snared.
One brought bishops on his shoulders,
50   One brought thieves, one brought soldiers,
Parsons, abbots, friars, monks,
Cardinals, knights, kings, and a whole bunch
Who died in the state of mortal sin
And in the end were taken in.
Devils came carrying the lost,
And there was Lucifer, their boss,
Who when he saw them with their stack,
Cried, "By my faith, you're welcome back.
You haven't been on holiday.
60   These folks will have a long, warm stay.
But looking over you, I fear
Not every one of us is here."
—"Yes, sir, we are," they said, "except
One lazy ninny who's inept
At salving consciences, soul-winning,
And tricking people into sinning."

At last the missing imp came straggling
In late with the dead jongleur dangling
Naked from his neck. Down
70   He threw the minstrel on the ground.
Satan addressed the prisoner.
"Boy," he said, "what are you in for?
Were you a thief, a crook, a smuggler?"
—"Nope," he answered, "just a jongleur.
Here's how I usually had to dress.
What you see is all my flesh
Wore on earth. I had to put up
With cold and people saying, 'Shut up!
Get out!' Now here's a place to stay!
80   Would you like to hear me play
A little song?" —"No. Songs won't do.
We'll find other work for you.
And since you're bare and badly clothed
We're going to have you stoke the stove."
—"Okay," he answered. "By Saint Peter,
I could use work near a heater."
One night the devils, congregated
Around the gates of Hell, awaited
Orders to rise and issue forth
90   And gather souls throughout the earth.
But first to the slave who night and morning
Kept the furnace fires burning,
Satan said, "Tonight we march.
Jongleur, I'm leaving you in charge
Of all my souls. I'll hold you liable,
Slit your nose, pluck out an eyeball,
And hang you live from your left ear
If one soul's lost while I'm not here."
—"Yes, sir," the jongleur said, "Go on.
100   I'll do my best here while you're gone.
You count on me. Don't be concerned.
I'll keep them safe till you've returned."
—"You'd better, boy. Don't let me down,
Because when I get back to town
If you have lost one single sinner
I'm going to eat you whole for dinner."
The jongleur hurried back to warming
Himself while up the imps rose swarming.
Well, now. Next I'm going to tell
110   How the jongleur managed Hell
And how Saint Peter managed, too.

Saint Peter came down, barging through
Hell Gate, into the underworld.
His beard was black, his mustache twirled.
Dressed to the nines and looking nice,
With his game table and three dice,
He quietly sat down beside
The jongleur keeping Hell and said,
"Friend, how about a little game?
120   See this fine table? Be a shame
To waste. See these three genuine
Square face straight shooters? You could win
Pounds of pounds sterling off of me
With these." He let the jongleur see
His coin purse filled with shining silver.
"Sir," said the jongleur, "by my liver,
By God and all his saints, I'm swearing,
All I've got's the shirt I'm wearing.
For God's sake, leave and let me stoke.
130   There's one thing certain: I'm flat broke."
—"My dear friend," said the saint, "I see
You've got some souls—bet two or three."
—"Hold on a minute, don't be funny!
Souls! If I lost even one, he
Would persecute me like a hive
Of bumble bees; he'd eat me live!"
Saint Peter answered, "Who's to know?
I won't tell. Ten souls or so
Won't be missed. Look here again:
140   Fresh-minted silver, yours to win!
The opportunity you're getting!
A hundred sous!—I'll start the betting!
You bet your souls instead of money."
     And when the jongleur saw so many
Silver coins shine before his eyes,
He coveted them, grabbed the dice,
And shouted to the saint, "Let's play!
I'm ready for you now. I lay
One soul against your sous for ante."
150   —"No, two souls, two! What kind of panty-
Waist game is this? And each by right
Can raise it one soul, black or white."
—"Okay," the jongleur said, "play on!"
—"Thank you, good. I raise you one."
—"Before the dice throw? What the devil?
Well, put your money on the table."

—"By God," Saint Peter said, "why not?"
And put some pounds into the pot.
They both sat down beside the furnace
160   And put their minds to dice in earnest.
"Let's not delay things any longer.
Your hands are clever: roll them, jongleur!"[1]
He rolled. Saint Peter said, "That eight
Is mine, the way I calculate.
If you throw hazard the next time,[2]
The three souls in the pot are mine."
Then he threw three and two and one.[3]
"You lost," Saint Peter said. —"Uh huh,"
The jongleur said, "but, damn, I'll fix
170   That soon. Here's three and three more—six!"
Saint Peter answered him, "Okay,"
Then threw the dice down right away.
Seventeen is what he got:
"You owe me nine now. Ha! I'm hot!"
—"Yeah," the jongleur said. "You win.
Uh, if I raise, will you stay in?"
Saint Peter answered, "Well, I guess so."[4]
—"Good. Nine against the nine I owe,
Plus three. Twelve more souls in the kitty."
180   —"Good. Damn whoever talks of quitting."
—"Then throw!" the jongleur said. —"Will do,"
Saint Peter answered, and he threw:
"Another hazard! Hazard—see!
You owe me eighteen plus the three."
—"Good God, I never," the jongleur swore,

---

[1] The jongleur will throw the entire round of this game.

[2] JO (p. 106) gives a succinct description of the rules of the dice game; they are playing at *hasard*: "Any one of the totals 18, 17, 16, 15, 6, 5, 4, or 3 constitutes a throw called *hasard*, and if this appears as the first throw of a round it is a winning one. If any one of the remaining totals from 14 to 7 inclusive appears at the first throw it is called a *chance* and is apportioned to the opponent. The thrower then throws again, and this time if he throws a *hasard* (technically called *re-hasard*), it is a losing throw, the opponent wins the round and handles the dice for the next round. Should the thrower after throwing one *chance* for his opponent, throw another *chance*, this is credited to himself [the thrower], and the round continues until either his own number comes up, in which case he wins, or his opponent's number, in which case the thrower loses...."

[3] The jongleur throws 8, a chance given to Saint Peter who wins three souls (l. 166). Then, the jongleur throws 6 (re-hasard) (l. 170).

[4] The stakes are doubled, with Saint Peter throwing. He throws hasard (l. 183) and wins 18 plus 3 souls, 21 souls.

"Heard of this happening before.
Tell me the truth, and in good faith:
How many dice are you playing with?
Or else what kind of loaded di—
190   Let's change the game. Let's play roll-high."[1]
—"Friend," the saint answered, "as you wish.
You want roll-high? Roll-high it is.
We'll play whatever pleases you.
High score for one throw or for two?"
—"One. One throw per bet is plenty.
Those twenty-one, plus one and twenty!"
Saint Peter shook the dice and crossed
Himself: "God help me!" Then he tossed:
"Seventeen! Wow, what a throw!
200   That's sixty souls you're going to owe!"
—"Wait. You're forgetting one small rule:
Both players have the right to roll."
The jongleur threw. The saint observed,
"Your dice roll isn't worth a turd.
Sorry, but your souls keep going.
On three dice you've got fifteen showing.
This isn't a bad day for me.
Now you owe me sixty-three."
—"Well, by the shroud God took a nap in,
210   A game like this just doesn't happen.
By all the saints that Rome has in it,
You can't convince me for one minute
The dice weren't loaded when you threw."
—"Go on and throw! What's wrong with you?"
—"I say you cheated! I know at least twice
You took your turn with loaded dice
Or changed the spots. You cheated. Cheater!"
And when he heard this charge, Saint Peter
Shouted, "That's a rotten damn
220   Lie! Just the kind of filthy scam
Scum try when they can't get their way:
'Somebody changed the dice,' they say.

---

[1] The jongleur proposes to change the game to roll-high: in one stroke of three dice, the higher total wins. In line 196, the stakes had been at 42: twenty-one from the initial win (ll. 178–79), and 21 won when Saint Peter threw hasard (l. 184). In line 200, Saint Peter, in anticipation of a win, is not counting the initial stake of 3 souls and looks forward to winning 60 souls. He will rectify the winnings (l. 208) after the jongleur has thrown a lower total (l. 206).

Why you're a low-down, deadbeat bleater.
What? Calling me a cheater,
Are you? Are you?: Cheater? Huh?
By God, I ought to break your jaw."
—"Yes, right," he answered, scorching for grief;
"I'm calling you a cheating thief,
Spoiling my game. Not one damn sous
230   You'll keep from me. You're trying to screw
Me out of what's mine with your crummy
Cheating. Come on, come take 'em from me!"
Then he jumped up and grabbed the cash.
Saint Peter jumped up too, and crash!—
Tackled the jongleur. Down they tripped.
Out of his hand the money slipped.
The jongleur roared for grief and reared
And gripped Saint Peter by the beard
And pulled his face across the floor.
240   Saint Peter poked him back and tore
The jongleur's shirt down to his belt.
Never had the jongleur felt
So ashamed as when he saw
His own pink skin exposed and raw.
They fought and kicked and poked and punched
And pinched and gouged and scratched so much
At last the jongleur had to face it:
All his blows and kicks were wasted,
The saint was bigger, tougher, stronger,
250   And if the fight went on much longer,
His clothes would be so stripped and strewed
Around, he might as well go nude.
"Sir," he suggested, "let's leave off.
Don't you believe we've quarreled enough?
Let's make friends again, sir, same
As before—How about another game
For friendship's sake?—if you'd be willing...."
—"You dared accuse me—me!—of stealing!
Huf! You got my liver heated,"
260   Saint Peter said, "when you said I cheated!"
—"I'm sorry. I was wrong. I promise
Not to say it again, sir, honest,
And woe is me," the jongleur said,
"Look at my clothes: they're shot to shreds.
Sir, you had all of the good hits,
So let's make up and call it quits."
—"Agreed," he said. Then they shook hands,

Kissed, hugged, and once again were friends.
"Friend," said Saint Peter, "listen to me.
270   You owe me some souls: sixty-three."
—"Sure," said the jongleur, "by Saint Jacques.
But now I know what my mistake was:
Shooting too early in the day—
Now's my time to win! Let's play.
Six score or nothing is the bet!"
—"Fine," Saint Peter said. "Bet! And yet ...,
Tell me, dear friend, will you be able
To pay me my souls without a squabble?"
—"Sure. Gladly. All. At your request.
280   What currency would you like best?
How about lords and ladies, priors,
Monks, thieves and warriors, sellers, buyers?
Which would you rather, men or women?
Priests or chaplains, serfs or yeomen?"
—"Now you're talking," Saint Peter answered.
—"Then roll the dice, but nothing fancy, sir."
Saint Peter rolled, but all his score
This time was three and a five and a four.
The jongleur shouted, "I see twelve!"
290   Saint Peter groaned: "I'm in a hell of
A grim predicament unless
Jesus helps me out of this mess,
'Cause that throw wasn't any good."
The jongleur threw as hard as he could:
A five, a two, and another five.[1]
"God," said Saint Peter, "still alive!
This tie may win me something yet.
Say, jongleur, friend, let's raise the bet:
Let's make the bet a dozen score!"
300   —"Suits me," the jongleur told him, "sure.
Twelve score souls it is. Now shoot!"
"I'm shooting, I'm shooting, by Saint Knute!"
Saint Peter shook the dice and shot
Two sixes and one little spot,
And then he shouted, "What a roll!
That one spot wins a pot of souls."
The jongleur cried, "One lousy point!
This guy has got me by the groin

---

[1] A tie. As JO points our (109) the rule for the tie-breaker is that the first thrower who exceeds 12 wins. Saint Peter throws 13 (l. 304) and wins.

And won't let loose. I never had
310   Any luck. It's always bad.
A wretch, a sucker, and a damn
Loser's what I was and am."
     Now when the spirits who were baking
Understood that he was staking
And losing them, "By Heaven's Lord,"
They shouted out with one accord
To Peter, "All our hope's in you!"
Saint Peter, answered, "Yes, that's true.
And mine in you, but if I'd tossed
320   Badly, our hope would have been lost.
God willing, soon, before day ends,
You will be one with me, my friends."
     There isn't much more of *The Jongleur*.
I will not make a short tale longer.
With every roll, Saint Pete would win,
Digging the jongleur deeper in,
Till all the souls were won from Hell
And ushered out in a great swell
To Paradise. The jongleur stayed,
330   Dismal, dejected and dismayed,
Wretched, repentant, on the rack.
     And now the imps came swarming back.
Lucifer walked in his door,
Looked around, then looked once more.
Back and forth his eyeballs roved,
In the ovens, on the stove.
He called the jongleur over: "Where
Are the souls entrusted to your care,
To watch and guard and keep in Hell?"
340   —"Sir, I was about to tell
You that. For God's sake, sir, have pity!
An old man broke into your city
With bags of money. My design
Was good—to make that money mine.
We played and played. He gave me credit
From your account of souls. I bet it
All away! Alas!" —"You bungler!
You son of a bitch! You jerk! You jongleur!
Your juggling's cost me! Where's the fiend
350   That brought him here? He'll pay!" They found
And caught and brought the one who'd stolen
And hauled the jongleur's sinful soul in.
They beat and kicked him till he swore

He'd never, ever, anymore
Haul any jongleurs down to Hell.
"Out of my house and my hotel!"
The master told the jongleur, "Scram!
Your juggling isn't worth a damn.
It lost my souls. Out! Take the stair.
360   Go to God for all I care!"
        The jongleur, when the Tyrant chased
Him out of the Inferno, raced
To heaven without hesitating.
Saint Peter stood at the gate, waiting.
As soon as he the jongleur spied,
He flung the gate of Heaven wide
And lodged him richly as a king.
        Now let all jongleurs feast and sing
For joy and clap their hands and shout,
370   Because the jongleur threw them out
Of torment when he threw the dice
And lost their souls to Paradise.

XIX   *The Three Hunchbacks*

The tale of the recalcitrant dead has fourteen versions which have spread over Europe and the Middle East. All fourteen have a communality of essential traits but differ in ornamental features such as the circumstances surrounding the presence of the bodies in the house.

The popularity of the general plot is attested by several similar fabliaux: *Estormi* (MR 1:198), *Des III Prestres* (MR 6:42), and other stories with the unwanted corpse theme. The humor of our tale lies in its incongruity and in its repetitive elements, the "absurdity of mistaking a live hunchback for a dead one" and the pacing of the story (Cooke, OF 47). For Thomas Cooke, the humor arises from the comic repetition "of the same act three times, each done with mounting exasperation," which "establishes the pattern that makes inescapable the disposal of the husband who shares an important accidental characteristic with the three minstrels" (OF 125). Bédier (246) had seen correctly the quasi-mathematical series of macabre events: "Tout le conte parait imaginé pour cet épisode final, si imprévu, si logique pourtant" (The whole tale seems to have been created for this surprising, yet so logical, final episode).

> My lords, if you will linger here
> A little while and lend an ear,
> I will relate a fabliau
> Of something that happened long ago.
> It's true, and furthermore it rhymes.
>   A burgher lived in former times,
> I don't recall exactly where,
> Douai perhaps, or near to there,
> Who lived in luxury and ease
> By selling off his properties.
> He was a man men liked to know.
> Although his cash was getting low,
> He always knew where he could get it:
> Rich bourgeois friends would give him credit;
> Soon he was everybody's debtor.
> He had a very lovely daughter,
> So beautiful it was a sin.
> Indeed, I think there's never been
> Created since the dawn of nature

10

20   A more exquisite, perfect creature.
     I don't know how—and no one does—
     To say how beautiful she was,
     So I'll say nothing. It won't do
     For me to say what's less than true.
         A humpback lived there in the town.
     An uglier wretch could not be found.
     His head was almost half his height.
     Nature must have worked all night
     To fashion him exactly wrong.
30   No two parts seemed to belong
     Together; all was ugliness.
     His head was big, his scalp a mess;
     His neck was short, his shoulders wide—
     They hugged his ears on either side.
     I'd be a fool to waste the day
     Trying and failing to convey
     His ugliness. His life he'd spent
     Collecting interest and rent,
     And if the story is correct,
40   This hunchback managed to collect
     Much too much money. They didn't come
     Richer than he; and that's the sum
     Of him and how he worked and lived.
         The father's friends agreed to give
     The daughter in the bloom of health
     To the hunchback for his wealth.
     But from the minute they were married,
     The hunchback husband fumed and worried
     Because of the beauty of his wife.
50   Jealousy controlled his life.
     Night after night he hardly slept.
     All day the door to his house he kept
     Tight shut. He sat there doing sentry
     Before the door, refusing entry
     To all who came, unless they'd come
     To pay him money or borrow some;
     Until one Christmas afternoon
     There came to him to ask a boon
     Beneath the landing where he rested
60   Three hunchback minstrels who requested
     That they might share his Christmas meal,
     For nowhere else could these three feel
     So comfortable; here they might find
     Festivity with their own kind,

Because he had a back like theirs.
He brought them up the outside stairs
To the front door and let them in.
Dinner was ready to begin.
A place was set for every guest.
70   The master, it must be confessed,
Served them a very hearty feast.
He wasn't tight, not in the least,
But made them welcome to partake
Of peas and bacon, capons, cake.
When they had eaten, before they left,
He gave them each a handsome gift
Of twenty Paris-minted sous,
And bidding them sincere adieus,
He warned them solemnly and swore
80   That if they ventured anymore
Within his house or in his yard
And they were caught, they'd find it hard
To have to bathe outside and shiver
In the cold waters of the river.
(The hunchback's mansion stood beside
A river that was deep and wide.)
When they had heard what he had to say,
Immediately they went away
Most willingly, and well content,
90   Considering that they had spent
A profitable evening there.
The lord went down the outside stair
Out to the bridge for a little walk.
His wife had heard the minstrels talk
And merrily sing in the room below.
She got a servant girl to go
And fetch them back to sing some more.
When they came in, she locked the door.
But as the guests stood entertaining
100 The lady with their glad refraining,
Here came the husband, who didn't care
To be too long away from there.
He tried the door and found it locked,
Called out her name and loudly knocked.
And by his voice she knew him well,
But for the world, she couldn't tell
What to do or how provide
A place for three hunchbacks to hide.
Over in a corner stood

110   A bed of heavy oaken wood,
        And in the bed three wooden chests.
        What shall I say? You'll hear the rest.
        In each, a hunchback had to hide.
        And when the master came inside,
        His wife, who knew his every whim,
        Felt obliged to sit by him.
        It wasn't very long before
        The husband rose, went out the door
        And left the house. She wasn't sorry.
120   She was, however, in a hurry
        To reassure her hunchback guests,
        Who still were hidden in the chests,
        And let them out, but she discovered
        A hunchback minstrel had been smothered
        In every chest she looked inside.
        She was completely horrified
        To find that all of them were dead.
        Out of the door the lady fled
        And cried to a porter passing near
130   And beckoned him and called, come here!
        When he had heard, as fast as he could,
        The porter ran to where she stood.
        "My friend," she said, "listen to me.
        If you will pledge me fealty
        And swear to keep what I say to you
        In confidence between us two,
        I guarantee your fortune's made:
        Thirty pounds you will be paid
        When you have carried out my order."
140   When he had heard her pleas, the porter
        Didn't hesitate to take
        Her offer, for the money's sake
        And for his eagerness and pride.
        He raced the stairs and came inside.
        "My friend," she said, "do not be nervous.
        If you would do me loyal service,
        Take this corpse to the river for me."
        She raised a lid for him to see
        And handed him a burlap sack.
150   He stuffed it with the dead hunchback,
        Shouldered the sack and quick as a hare,
        Ran out the door and down the stair,
        Then up along the water's edge
        And halfway out across the bridge,

And dropped the hunchback in the water.
Not taking any time to loiter,
Back to the hunchback's house he hustled.
       The lady there at last had wrestled
A second corpse from the bed of death
160   And was completely out of breath
From the hard work that she had done.
She moved from where she'd put him down.
       Elated now, the man returned:
"Pay me," he told her, "what I've earned.
Your dwarf is carried off and sunk."
—"Sir Dolt," she said, "you must be drunk.
You can't pull wool over my eyes.
The dwarf's not taken. Here he lies.
You stopped at the street, emptied the sack,
170   Then brought both sack and hunchback back.
Look over there if you think I'm lying."
—"What the devil? Well for crying—
How did the dead man climb the stairs?
Somehow he took me unawares.
That man was dead; that I could tell.
This is some Antichrist from Hell.
But by St. Ralph, his tricks won't work!"
He seized the hunchback with a jerk,
Shoved him headfirst in the sack,
180   Hoisted him upon his back
And down the steps to the river ran.
       The lady dragged the third dead man
Out of the chest where he had died
And set him by the fireside,
Then went to wait above the street.
       The porter grabbed the hunchback's feet
And hurled him headlong in the river.
"Be gone!" he shouted, "Damn your liver
If you return here anymore."
190   He hurried back to the lady's door,
Demanding that he get his pay
Without excuses or delay.
She said she'd gladly pay his hire,
Then led him upstairs to the fire
As if she didn't know about
The third hunchback, whom she'd laid out.
"Look!" she exclaimed, "What a surprise!
A miracle before our eyes.
That hunchback's lying there again!"

200 The young man wasn't laughing then
At the hunchback by the fireplace.
"Look here," he cried, "God's holy face!
This minstrel really takes the cake.
Will all I do today be take
This cursed hunchback to the river
And find him here again whenever
I come upstairs to get my cash?"
Into the sack he had to stash
The third hunchback. Enraged and grieved,
210 He seized the heavy sack and heaved
It to his neck. About he faced
And hot with indignation raced
Down to the riverbank to sink
Another hunchback in the drink.
"Go back to Hell, you wretched stiff!
I've carried you so much that if
You venture here again, you'll rue
The moment I catch sight of you.
I'm pretty sure you have me hexed,
220 But by the lord high God, when next
I see you sneaking on my trail,
And I can find a stick or flail,
I'll give you such a knock in the head,
The gash you get will be bright red."
     The porter, having made this speech,
Left the bridge, but didn't reach
The hunchback's doorway with his sack
Before he happened to turn back
And see the husband coming after.
230 This didn't move the man to laughter.
He crossed himself and double crossed:
"*Nomine Patris*, Son and Ghost!"[1]
(He was upset, no *if*'s and *maybe*'s.)
"Lord help," he said, "this corpse has rabies,
Dogging my heels the livelong night.
He's almost close enough to bite.
Damnation strike me if he doesn't
Take me for a stupid peasant
Who doesn't know his way around.
240 Is his idea of fun to hound

---

[1] Latin for "In the name of the Father." In the original, the porter only uses the first word in Latin: "Nomini Dame Diex" (In the name of the Lord God).

Me everywhere I take myself?"
He ran inside and from a shelf
Seized a huge pestle and once more
Came charging out of the front door.
The lord was on the first step then.
"What Mr. Hunchback! Back again?
You're a stiff, die-hard cadaver,
But by God's mother, and the Father,
Crossing my path again was crazy.
250   You think I'm recreant or lazy?"
He lifted up the pestle, charged,
Hit the lord's head, which was too large,
And gave it such a mighty clout,
The blood and brains came pouring out.
There on the step the hunchback died.
The porter put the corpse inside
The sack, securely tied the top,
Then off he ran and didn't stop
Till he had dumped the fourth hunchback
260   Off the bridge, still in the sack
Because he feared the corpse might swim
Back to the bank and follow him.
"Begone," he said, "go back to Hell,
And I can honestly foretell
As long as grass grows in the country,
You won't be coming back to haunt me."
He ran to the lady right away,
Demanding that she quickly pay
His money, which he'd worked so much
270   To earn, nor did the wife begrudge
Whatever pay the man demanded.
Thirty pounds, no less, she handed
Over to him and still could feel
She had the better of the deal.
And when she paid him, she agreed
He'd done good work, for he had freed
Her from her lord, that ugly dwarf.
All her long life from that day forth
Never another care had she
280   Once widowhood had set her free.
        Durand, who fashioned this, has stated
That never yet has God created
A girl whom money couldn't get,
And furthermore, the Lord has yet
To fashion goods, however good,

Which, if the truth were understood,
A sum of money couldn't buy.
The hunchback, though the price was high,
Bought him a wife, that lovely girl.
290   Shame on the man, be he knight or churl,
Who lives for money, which is cursed,
And shame on the man who coined it first.

Amen

XX   *The Sacristan Monk*

The tales of the "Long Night" were very popular. Indeed, no fewer than eight versions of this tale have come down to us. They are, in fact, made up of two different themes joined one to the other: in order to have an "unwanted corpse" one needs a body! Thus, a seduction theme initiates the theme of the "Dead Man Killed Several Times Over" (see *The Three Hunchbacks*).

The difficulty for the author is to manage to make a killer not only unpunished but also likeable. Thus, it is important to show us the victim as ignoble and the killer as unlucky as possible. The latter is down on his luck, left ruined and indebted by robbers, while the former despicably takes advantage of his misfortune and propositions the virtuous wife in church, during her prayers, right by the altar (ll. 94–138; 228–48) and steals the bribe money from the monastery coffers and the poorboxes (ll. 251–54). At the end, when the monk ends up at the abbey which he should have never left, we feel satisfied that the circle is closed and don't feel unduly sorry for the victim. Indeed, the true victim is Sire Tibu, who has lost his bacon!

This tale has been lauded for its well-prepared episodes and excellent motivation of actions which lead to a satisfying climax (OF 133; M 48). Cooke notes that the monk visits every locale at least twice, reappearing like an inopportune ghost. To provide variety within repetition, the author introduces different discoverers and different circumstances for each rediscovery of the corpse (OF 133).

> And now I'll tell a monk's life story:
> The Sacristan of a monastery
> Loved a merchant's wife, for she
> Was rich in honor and courtesy.
> The name of the lady was Ydwanne;
> Her husband's, Will the businessman.
> Ydwanne was gracious, good and kind,
> Beautiful, well bred, refined.
> William knew his business well,
> Worked hard for his money and always dealt
> Honorably with all he met,
> And wasn't constantly in debt
> At any of the bars or taverns.
> His cupboards, full and deep as caverns,

10

Were open to his many guests.
Beggars he didn't treat like pests,
But gave them what they asked, and double.
They were a very wealthy couple.
    But Satan, who is never napping,
20   Worked hard to find a way of trapping
And testing them beyond their power.
Finally, William had to borrow,
Because his capital was spent
On his investments. First he went
To get a loan at Provinstown's
Biennial fair, of eighty pounds
In Provins-minted coins. And then
He took his money to Amiens
And bought fine cloths. Then home he started,
30   Triumphant, carefree, and light-hearted
Because he'd bought the fabric cheap.
But thieves and thugs, who never sleep,
Kept watch at every woodland track.
His fellow merchants hurried back
Two days before him. He stayed late
Because he wished to celebrate.
At last, with serving man and goods,
He set out. Soon they reached the woods
Where robbers lay in wait, eyes peeled
40   For businessmen from whom to steal.
As soon as they could see him coming,
From all directions they came running,
Seized him and knocked him off his horse,
But hadn't harmed him any worse,
Except to take his cloth and gear,
When suddenly his man appeared,
Following his dog. The thieves
Fell upon him with their knives.
William watched till his man was dead
50   From bleeding; then he turned and fled
Far as his tired legs allowed.
Where were all his profits now?
Those people who had loaned the sack
Of cash to him would want it back
When he got back. And when he did,
They asked him, "Who are you trying to kid?
Don't we have your IOU?
I want my money! Pay what's due!"
—"Gentlemen, gentlemen, gentlemen, wait!

60   I have three windmills, working late
        And early making flour. Please,
        Don't be anxious. Leave me in peace.
        Take my mills until I pay."
        The men agreed and went away,
        Glad to get the deal of their life.
            William went home and told his wife,
        A lady full of grace and charm.
        When she reacted with alarm,
        He sweetly reasoned with her: "Dear,
70   Don't be angry. What's to fear?
        Even though our Lord's permitted
        All our savings to be looted,
        Even though I feel forsaken
        By God when all my goods are taken,
        God exists among us still.
        He'll counsel us, if that's his will."
        —"I don't know what to say, my lord,"
        His wife replied. "I am disturbed
        Deeply by our loss. And why
80   Did that poor servant have to die?
        But you're alive, so I don't care.
        People often do repair
        Lost wealth. No one brings back the dead."
            They talked late. Then they went to bed.
        Next morning, to the monastery
        She went, to pray the son of Mary,
        After whom the church was named.
        She lit a candle. By its flame
        She prayed, "Lord, tell me what to do . . .
90   And help him get his wealth back, too."
        She placed the candle on the altar.
        Stars glittered in her eyes. She faltered
        In her prayer, sighing, crying.
        The Sacristan was nearby, spying.
        He had adored her long and greatly.
        Now he approached her: "Hello, lady.
        Welcome to our little cloister."
        —The lady wiped her eyes, unflustered
        By his approach. "Sir," she replied,
100   "May you find favor in God's eyes."
        —"Favor? The favors of your fair
        Body in bed for me to share
        In secret," said the Sacristan,
        "Are all the favors I demand!

May all the years I've spent in wishing
And making plans now reach fruition.
Ydwanne, I am the monastery
Treasurer. I'll pay you very
Substantially: a hundred pounds—
110   You'll live in style in new silk gowns."
      A hundred pounds! That much temptation
Deserved a little consideration.
"Should I accept them," Ydwanne wondered.
That would be quite a gift. A hundred
Pounds would go far. But she was still
In love with her dear husband, Will.
She told herself she would receive
Nothing without her husband's leave.
      The monk returned to his motif:
120   "Lady, you don't know the grief
You've put me through. You've made me sweat.
For four long years I loved you, yet
Never laid hands on you until
This very moment. Now I will!"
He grabbed her, pulled her, kissed her smack
On the mouth by force! Ydwanne pulled back:
"Good sir! What are you thinking of?
Church is no place for making love.
I'm going home to ask advice
130   About you from my husband." —"Nice!
Nice thinking!" said the monk. "I wish you
Wouldn't consult him on this issue."
—"Don't be afraid," she said. "It's funny
What people will endure for money.
I'll trick him into trying to
Convince me to comply with you."
The monk pulled out his purse and shook
Ten sous out, which the lady took.
She took the sous, then home she fled,
140   Home, where there was no salt or bread,
Because they'd sunk from rich to poorest,
Because her husband, through the forest,
Had taken their wealth and lost it all.
At home she spoke, and he kept still.
"William," she told him, "listen to me.
I have a plan. If you agree,
I swear that by two years from now
You will be rich." —William asked, "How?"
Ydwanne reached out. From hand to hand

150   She poured the sous the Sacristan
       Had given her. He welcomed them
       Into his hands and counted: ten.
           Ydwanne went on: "Dear husband, Will,
       For the love of God, don't take it ill
       If I reveal some private business."
       Then she told from start to finish
       How the Sacristan waylaid
       Her in the abbey church and prayed
       And promised her a hundred pounds.
160   William laughed and swore: "That sounds
       Disgusting! Not for all the treasure
       Of Caesar and Nebuchadnezzar
       Would I allow you to contract
       'Private business' on your back!
       I'd rather go hungry—beg for my bread
       All my life. I'd rather be dead."
       The lady heard how he protested.
       Then she pleasantly suggested:
       "Yes, sir, you're right, but couldn't people
170   Who schemed with skill and didn't scruple
       To execute a clever plan
       By which to clip the Sacristan
       Arrange things so all ended well?
       One thing's sure—he wouldn't tell
       The Abbot or the Prior on us."
       —"No ... you're not kidding. ... What a bonus
       A hundred pounds would add up to.
       Think of the good that it would do!
       It's worth a try at least, Ydwanne,"
180   Said William; "do you have a plan?"
       —"Yes, and here it is, so pay
       Attention, William: I'll go pray
       At church tomorrow morning early
       Before Saint Martin's altar. Surely
       I'll get to see the Sacristan,
       And then I'll tell him, if I can,
       To come to me as stipulated
       In the proposal he related
       To me today. Don't worry—he'll come
190   Willingly and bring the sum
       He promised he would bring to me."
       —"Good," her husband said, "we'll see.
       God damn whoever backs out now."
       —"I won't," she said. "you have my vow."

—"Lady, it's late," he said. "I think
We ought to talk about food and drink
For supper." —"Yes, you're right," she said;
"You go buy some meat and bread,
Whatever kind of meat you choose."
200   She sent him off with the ten sous.
He hurried to the stalls and shops
And bought a dozen mutton chops
And brought them home to her. The woman
Sent a boy to buy some cummin,
Some pepper, and a jug of wine.
She made the sauce, and then they dined
Together with great love and joy
And no one with them but the boy.
Well they drank, and well they ate,
210   Then went to bed, since it was late.
And there they hugged and cooed and purred
And kissed and didn't speak the word
"Poor" or say, "There's not enough";
Having each other, they were well off,
As in each other's arms they lay.
        Ydwanne arose at break of day.
She put her shoes on and got dressed,
Pulled back her hair and tied her best
Silken wimple on her head.
220   Then off to church the lady sped.
When she arrived, she had to wait
For those who'd been to celebrate
The morning mass and were already
Coming out again. The lady
Waited a moment; then she went
Straight to the statue of the saint,
And there she stopped to kneel in prayer.
The monk peered out ... Was she there?
She was! How pleased her presence made him.
230   He hastily approached her: "Madam,
You took so long! Why the delay?
Tell me, what's in your heart today?
My body feels like it's been beaten.
I haven't drunk, I haven't eaten
Since we talked. I'm going crazy!"
—"There, there. Be calm," replied the lady;
"You'll have the comfort and delight
Of me in bed this very night,
Given the terms that we discussed."

240   —"Oh, yes, my lady. Put your trust
       In me. One hundred pounds I'll bring
       And more. I must: there's not a thing
       On earth I ask except to play
       And sport with you from dusk to day.
       As mighty God's my testimony,
       When next we meet, I'll bring the money."
       The Sacristan gave her a little
       More money now to buy some victuals.
       They said goodbye, and then they parted.
250   She went back home, and the monk started
       Searching through the monastery's
       Coffers, altars, sanctuaries,
       Poorboxes, and containers where
       People leave money during prayer.
       Into his money belt he stuffed
       All he could find. He hadn't bluffed
       When he had said one hundred pounds.
       If any further had been found,
       The lady surely would have got it.
260   Poor son of a bitch! Gladly he plotted
       His own undoing, while the lady
       Got an early supper ready
       For her husband, who soon slunk
       To bed, to wait there for the monk,
       With a churl's thick club beneath the cover.
            Now the evening prayers were over,
       Compline chanted, and the monks[1]
       Gone to their dormitory bunks—
       Except one monk, who lagged behind.
270   Sleep wasn't what he had in mind.
       Love was all he thought about.
       Silently, secretly, he slipped out
       The postern gate. Then he walked
       Quickly to William's house and knocked,
       According to the plan he'd hatched.
       After she let him in, she latched
       The door and said, "Just you and me!"
       (But William, in the bed, made three.)
       The monk ate dinner and drank wine
280   With Will's beloved wife, Ydwanne,
       Whose company would cost him plenty.

---

[1] Compline: liturgical prayer for the close of day.

"My dear, sweet friend," Ydwanne asked gently,
"Where's my money?" —"Here, it's yours,"
The monk replied; "it's in this purse.
Take it. One hundred pounds. Here, keep it.
I wouldn't lie. You think I'm stupid?"
She stowed the money in the closet,
Then happened to see the monk deposit
Beside the fire, in a chair,
290 His set of keys.... Oh, she was fair,
So beautiful he hurt all over.
He rose and started to manoever
Her to the hearth to get her hot.
"Dear God!" she said, "sir, have a thought
For people passing by the window.
Think of the trouble we'll get into!
Carry me to the bedroom, please,
Where you can fool with me at ease."
When he heard that, he got up, galled
300 And grieving at the way she stalled,
And rushed her to the room and laid
Her down face up upon the bed.
William slithered out from under.
"What's this?" he shouted. "Monk, by thunder,
I'll teach you what a fool you were
To try to make my wife your whore.
I'll be damned if I stand by
And let you do it. I'd rather die,
Damn you, then let you be her lover!"
310 When he heard that, the monk jumped off her
And tried to get the first blow in.
But William clubbed him in the chin
And knocked him senseless, then before
He could recover, struck once more.
The monk's brains spattered and his blood streamed.
Down he fell as William screamed,
"That's how fools chase after death!"
Ydwanne cried out and caught her breath
And sighed and wept: "What have you done?
320 I wish I were in Babylon
Or not been born or lived to see
This murder—on account of me!
Alas," she cried. "Oh William, William,
For God's sake, why did you have to kill him?"
—"I couldn't help it! I was scared.
That monk was big. He was prepared

To hit me. What did you want? Him nice
And comfortable between your thighs?
We've got to get away! We've got
330   To flee this country, find some spot
Where no one knows us or can hunt
Us down!" —"My lord," she said, "we can't.
The city gates are shut. Patrols
Walk upon the outer walls."
Ydwanne wept and William thought.
(When a fool thinks, beware the result!)
After he thought, he raised his head,
Looked at her solemnly, and said,
"My dear, which door did the monk take
340   Out of the abbey?" —"He took the gate
Behind the abbey. Will, look there.
He dropped his key—there, on the chair."
With a white cloth William bound
The monk's crushed head. Then he bent down,
Hoisted the corpse up and went out
With her behind him: she wasn't about
To stay in there alone, not even
If he were to cut her throat for leaving.
Near to the street she took her station.
350   William had the situation
Under control. In a hurry
He reached the gate to the monastery
Back yard, put down the Sacristan,
Unlocked it, picked him up again,
Went up a path where a monk or priest
Customarily came and pissed,
And found a chamber with some holes,
Used for relieving swollen bowels.
Upon a hole he set the monk.
360   Beside the door he saw a hunk
Of piled up hay and straw and grasses
With which the clerics wiped their asses.
William had been brought up right.
He took a wad and wrapped it tight
In the monk's fist. Then out he sped,
Away by another road that led
Him home again, still scared and shaking,
To his Ydwanne, who stood there waiting,
Just as shaken, just as scared.
370   They went inside, caressed and cared
And calmed each other. They no more shivered,

Believing they had been delivered
From the monk whom they had killed.
   Jaw hanging down, the monk sat still,
Upon his hole. The other monks
Slept on in their dormitory bunks.
In a separate bed the Prior lay
By the refectory. That day
He'd eaten too much and couldn't wait
380   To get up and evacuate.
Fast to the outhouse door he trotted.
At the first hole he reached, he squatted,
Eager to relieve himself.
He sat and strained and sat a spell.
At last he looked up and observed
The Sacristan, who, being murdered,
Didn't move a hand or foot.
"Ugh!" he whispered. "What a brute
This Sacristan is, sleeping here.
390   Tomorrow morning he'll pay dear
Between assembly and dismissal.
If he had slept through the epistle
He couldn't have shown less decorum."
The Prior rose and stood before him.
"Sir Sacristan," the Prior said,
"Use a dormitory bed
For sleeping, not a shithouse plank.
You shame your order and your rank,
Lowering yourself to this.
400   I'd burn my back and break my wrist
Rather than sleep in such a filthy,
Vile place." When he had said his fill, the
Prior approached the Sacristan,
Shouting, "Wake up! Wake up, man!"
But being fully dead, the monk
Fell sideways on the plank—ker-thunk!
And when he saw the corpse fall down,
"Holy Ghost, what's going on?"
The Prior yelled; "this monk is dead!
410   I've made a big mistake. Why did
I mess with him? Why didn't I stay
In bed? Oh God! And yesterday
We got into an argument!
The monks heard us. They'll say I went
And murdered him. They'll tell the Abbot!"
Scared and shaking like a rabbit,

He groaned, "Lord, tell me what to do!"
He thought and thought and decided to
Carry the body into town
420   Upon his back and lay it down
At the front porch of the most admired,
Gracious, courtly, and desired
Wife of the local bourgeoisie.
That morning everyone would see
And reason, "There's where he was murdered."
So now the Prior stooped and shouldered
The Sacristan, turned round and bore
Him to the house where earlier
The monk took poison whose effect
430   No antidote will counteract.
William, be wary! Heed my warning:
If people find him in the morning,
The game is up; William, you're dead.
    Ydwanne and William lay in bed,
Frightened and comforting each other.
There was a sudden change of weather,
The wind picked up and a strong gust
Caught the monk's robe, rocked him, and thrust
Him onto the door. Ydwanne heard *thupp*
440   And cried out, "William, lord, get up!
Someone's out there, by Saint Jonas.
He's been there all night, spying on us!"
William leaped up, grabbed his stick,
Raced across the room, and quick
Turned the key and flipped the latch.
The Sacristan, who had been bashed
To death, pitched forward through the door,
Bowling him backward to the floor.
And when he realized he had fallen,
450   Startled and scared, he started calling:
"Help! What happened? What's going on?
Come and help me quick, Ydwanne.
If this thing's human that just fell
On me, God damn my soul to hell
If he gets out of here alive."
Naked from the bed, his wife
Leaped and rushed to the fire side,
Lifted a torch and looked and cried,
"William, we've been betrayed. That man
460   On top of you is the Sacristan!"
—"Good God, you aren't mistaken, Honey.

Curses on ill-gotten money,
Cheating, greed, and dirty dealing!
No good can ever come of stealing!
But is he dead?" —"Of course he is!"
They scratched their heads and said, "Gee whiz,
How'd he get here?" till they were certain
He'd been transported back by Satan.
As William lifted the Sacristan,
470   She made for him a talisman
With God's name on it in big letters.
That made him feel a little better.
    He walked a while with the dead monk
Until he reached a pile of dung,
The property of Sir Tibu,
The tenant farmer, the man who grew
All the monastery's wheat,
Who drank good wine and ate good meat,
Whose purse was full, whose house was big.
480   Recently he'd killed a pig
Inside the house and hung the bacon
Up to dry. It had been taken
By a sly thief the night before.
The only place the thief could store
The meat securely was the dung.
    William came carrying the monk.
Tired from having born the load
All the way through town, he slowed,
And when he reached the dung heap, stopped.
490   He wondered if he couldn't drop
The body off a little early.
Then he decided he would bury
It in the dung and turn around
And go back home. Onto the ground
He flung the corpse. Then with his hands
He dug a hole where the Sacristan's
Dead body could be hid, but he touched
The bacon that the thief had filched.
He saw the skin! And it was black!
500   He scraped some more of the dung back
And figured, "This must be another
Black Benedictine monk's cadaver,
Blacker, though, than ordinary.
I think it would be best to bury
The monks together in one tomb."
He tried, but couldn't quite make room

For the new body. "By Saint Lot,
What am I going to do? This plot
Won't hold both. Now let me view
510   This other monk somebody slew."
He pulled the bacon loose. "By Pete,"
He said, "this isn't monk, it's meat!
Those forest robbers who attacked
Me took my tail, but I've got back
Bacon and a lot of money."
He put the monk inside the gunny
Sack, covered him completely in
The dung heap where the meat had been,
And took off running with the meat.
520   His wife was waiting on the street.
She saw the load and asked the man,
"William, is that the Sacristan
Again?" —"No, by St. Lucy!
This is a bacon, big and juicy.
I got the meat. You get some cabbage."
    Meanwhile, the rascal who had ravaged
The tenant farmer of his bacon
Was gambling in a bar, not slaking
His thirst, though he had wine to drink.
530   "Hey, my lords, what do you think
We ought to do," he asked his friends;
"If only we could lay our hands
On a big slab of roasted meat,
The wine would be a nicer treat
And go down better." Then each one swore
By eyes and ears, "How right you are!
But, friend, you might as well forget it.
We're out of cash, we can't get credit,
And all the butchers are in bed."
540   —"It just so happens," the thief said,
"I have a juicy, fat, first-rate
Slab of bacon I'll donate.
It's Sir Tibu's. I've stolen it
And hid it in a pile of shit."
—"Then get it. What are you waiting for?"
    He who had stolen goods galore
Hurried to the dung heap hole,
Looking for the meat he stole,
Dug up the monk, still in the sack,
550   Heaved him up, and hurried back
Into the tavern. Down he flung

The sack that he had dug from dung.
"Welcome, Welcome!" cried the crowd.
—"Oof, lords," he answered, "what a load!"
Then they all shouted, "Hey, come here!"
To the barmaid, Guenevere:
"Guenevere, got any sticks
Around that we can use to fix
A fire with, to cook delicious
560   Charbroiled bacon? How about the dishes?
Are they clean? Quick!" they cried;
"We're going to look for wood outside."
While Guenevere ran all around
Doing their bidding, they went and found
A fence constructed of thick, sturdy
Wooden stakes. Then everybody
Yanked out a stake and hurried back.
"Guenevere, get us an ax,"
They called. She brought it, washed the pan
570   That she would cook the meat in, ran
Like a woman gone berserk,
Tore open the bag, and with a jerk
Seized the body by a boot,
Sawed and sawed, but couldn't cut
A morsel off. —"Would you believe
That lazy bitch?" remarked the thieves.
"What's she ever good for? Nothing."
The barmaid heard the thieves' badmouthing
And answered back, "By St. Bernard,
580   You shut your mouths! This bacon's hard
As hangman's rope. And it's got shoes on,
That's what I think." Then in confusion
They all leaped up and shouted, "Shoes?"
And ran to the barmaid to peruse
The corpse, which still was in the sack.
The man who had brought it on his back
Crossed himself too fast for counting.
The barkeep, meanwhile, started shouting,
"Garnot, why'd you kill this monk?"
590   —"I didn't, sir," he said; "that's bunk.
I never touched him! It was Satan!
He must have conjured monk from bacon!
I swear to God, as God may give
Me good confession while I live,
That monk was bacon when I grabbed it.
It's Satan in disguise. The habit

Is meant to lure us down to hell.
But I can counteract the spell:
I'll pick him up and take him back
600   To Tibu's house." —"Good. Then make tracks,
And when you get there, hang the monk
From the same rope where the meat hung."
—"I will, by all the saints. Amen."
He picked the body up again
And set out boldly with his burden.
As he was running past a garden
Near the farmer's house, an old
Wheelbarrow caught his eye. He rolled
The barrow up against the wall
610   Of Tibu's house. Then up he crawled,
Reached the hole he'd made (through which
The slab of bacon had been snitched),
Shoved the burden that he bore
In through the hole, tied the cord
Tight to the corpse's neck, then dropped
To the ground, ran, and didn't stop
Till he was drinking with his gang,
Telling them how he had hanged
The monk where bacon once had been.
620   Let's leave the drinkers at the inn.
And now I'd like to speak to you
About the farmer, Sir Tibu,
Still asleep as dawn was breaking.
His wife was in the bed, too, waking.
"It's morning, sir," the lady said;
"We're down to just two loaves of bread—
Good time for going to the mill."
—"Lady," he answered, "I've been ill
Three days. Wake Martin up. He'll go.
630   I mean the peddler here, you know,
Who comes and spends the night here twice
Or three times every month. Be nice,
And promise him a loaf of bread."
—"All right.... Martin! Get out of bed!"
—"Lady," the peddler asked, "what for?"
—"To run to the mill! We're out of flour."
—"What?" he said. "You must be kidding.
Why should I rush to do your bidding?
The other day you killed a pig
640   And never offered me a big
Fat pork chop, tripes, or even a bone.

Do you suppose because you own
The straw I sleep on I'm your hound?
There's not a house for miles around
Where people wouldn't offer me
More loans and gifts, more willingly,
Than I get on this crummy place!"
—"Martin," she said, "don't make a case
Out of this. If I let you have
650   A big hunk of my bacon slab
And bread with butter on the slices,
Then, would you kindly be so nice as
To rise and go running to the mill?"
—"Lady," he said, "indeed I will,
Gladly, since you're being fair."
—"It's only right you get your share
Of bacon, and you will," she said.
She struck her husband: "Out of bed,
My lord!" she shouted; "Up! Arise!
660   Go and get some bacon. Slice
Some off for Martin. If we grill
It for him, he'll go to the mill."
The farmer climbed up toward the loft,
And called, "How much should I cut off?"
—"Cut where you please. Use your discretion.
Don't ask such a stupid question.
It's less my meat then it is yours."
—"That's right," he said. "It is. Of course.
Fetch me some fire to see it by."
670   —"Fetch you fire!" she answered. "Why?
You know where the bacon's hung!"
So Tibu had to grope among
The rafters till he thought he put
His hand on bacon, but the monk's foot
Was what he reached. And when he tried
To slice, the rope was so old, dried,
And smoked, it broke. Down the monk tumbled
On Tibu's head. Tibu crumpled
Into a box where wood was stored.
680   And when he realized he was floored,
"Martin, Martin," he cried, "awaken!
Get up! I'm in the box. The bacon
Fell on me!" Martin jumped and, quick,
Grabbed from the fire a flaming stick,
And by the flickering of the torch,
He saw Tibu and the monk's corpse.

He crossed himself ten times and more.
"By Saint Martin's cloak," he swore,
"This isn't bacon, sir: it's Satan,
690   Dressed like a monk, all shorn and shaven,
And on his cloven hoofs are shoes!
Damn it! Why did we have to lose
Our slab of bacon for a monk!"
—"Oh, God," Tibu said, "God, I'm sunk.
Tomorrow everyone will take
Me out and hang me by mistake.
They'll say I killed the Sacristan!"
—"Sir, sir," said Martin, "buck up, man!
Your moaning isn't worth a fart.
700   You'd better think instead, and start
To figure out some way to carry
This body to the monastery
Where it belongs. I'd like to strangle
Whoever got us in this tangle
And hang him from a birch or maple!"
—"Martin," he said, "go to the stable
And get my colt and some stout cord.
If I can tie this corpse aboard
A horse, we'll make the monk a knight."
710   Martin brought the colt, and tight
They tied the monk's feet to the stirrups.
Then Martin said, "God's holy cherubs!
I'll bring a beanpole from the house
And tie it to him. Let him joust
Down in the courtyard with his lance,
And you shout, 'Help! The Sacristan's
Stolen my colt. Sound the alarm!'"
They drove the colt out off the farm,
And the farmer cried, as loud as he could,
720   "Help, help!" and roused the neighborhood.
A hundred people chased the monk,
Thinking he was mad or drunk,
And the colt zigged, zagged, circled, then straight
She scampered through the abbey gate.
The Sacristan, with shield tied on,
Met the Subprior, up at dawn
(Who should have stayed in bed and slept)
And struck him with his lance and swept
Him off his palfrey. Then the crowd
730   Was flabbergasted, and they cried,
"Look out! Get back! The Sacristan

Has gone berserk. Back! Don't just stand
And wait for him to kill you! Run!"
Some were weak, some strong, but none
Stood fast. They bolted helter-skelter,
Everyone of them, for shelter
And locked the doors. But the colt crashed
In through the kitchen door and smashed
Pitchers and plates, glasses and platters,
740   Tables and chairs, and the shield battered
The wall incessantly a hundred
Times at least, and the lance was sundered.
Finally the commotion died
And the colt went wandering off outside
And reached a gully, broad and deep.
She braced herself so hard to leap,
The saddlegirths broke. Then she jumped
Not far enough. Down in one lump
Fell monk and colt. Men hauled him out
750   With hooks of iron. He didn't shout,
Because he was already dead.
        And that's how Will came out ahead
Against the wily Sacristan,
Who bartered for his wife, Ydwanne
(Will won a hundred pounds and bacon,
Got off scot-free, was never taken,
And wasn't even once accused);
And how the farmer had to lose
His bacon, and his colt was spilled;
760   And how the Sacristan was killed.